BOOK OF SOULS

A PROF CROFT PREQUEL NOVELLA

BRAD MAGNARELLA

THE PROF CROFT SERIES

PREQUELS
Book of Souls
Siren Call

MAIN SERIES
Demon Moon
Blood Deal
Purge City
Death Mage
Black Luck
Power Game
Druid Bond
Night Rune
Shadow Duel
Shadow Deep
Godly Wars
Angel Doom

SPIN-OFFS
Croft & Tabby
Croft & Wesson

MORE COMING!

1

My heart thumped hard and high in my chest as I sealed the door onto a pulsating blackness.

Turning, I snapped on my flashlight. Through a suspension of dust, bookcases loomed from the too-close walls. At the far end of the room, a large steamer trunk and an antique desk leaned in and out of the shadows, the desk featuring an old lamp with a blood-red shade and brass pull chain.

As I stepped from the door, the fear that had been balling up my insides let out, allowing a euphoric excitement to seep in. An entire life lived in this house, thirteen years to the day, and I had never been inside Grandpa's attic study. I was in unchartered territory.

Even better, forbidden territory.

I ran my beam over the titles on the bookshelves. An old encyclopedia set, row after row of books on insurance and insurance law. Boring titles, but my proximity to them made the hair on my arms tingle straight. Maybe it was because I knew almost nothing about my grandfather, a man who was rarely home, who rarely spoke even when he was. A man whose dour eyes and foreign accent scared the hell out of my friends—and me, if I was being honest.

I trained my beam on his trunk. A large, battered container of black wood and metal that looked for all the world like a pirate's chest. I undid both hasps and worked my fingernails around the edge of the central lock, surprised when the spring-loaded latch fell open.

A shot of anticipation jiggled my bladder. I clamped the flashlight between shoulder and cheek, placed my hands on the front of the lid ... and hesitated. As freaky as it sounded, the trunk felt alive. And it wasn't just the warmth of the pliant wood. A force was moving through my hands, a steady rising and falling, like breathing. And was that a heart beat?

My own heart lurched as I spun from the trunk. No, not a heart beat—footsteps, on the attic stairs. Their steady cadence accompanied by wooden taps now, growing louder.

Shit. Grandpa.

I replaced the hatch, refastened the hasps, and shot my beam around the study. A closet! In five jerky steps, I was plunging into a line of hanging coats and pulling the folding door closed behind me. A beat later, just as I snapped off my light, the study door creaked open and then closed again.

A heavy silence followed. I held my breath, sure Grandpa could sense my presence.

He uttered one of his strange words: *"Serrare."* Pressure built in my ears as the floorboards clicked and a dangling bulb flooded the room with weak light. I stiffened in my crouch. Grandpa's tall figure entered my view through the seam above the closet door's middle hinge, his back to me. I released my breath and blinked to moisten my eyes again.

Though the man usually carried himself like a ruler, his shoulders sloped now, as though bearing a large load. He set his cane and fedora on the desk and, sighing, ran a hand through his thinning hair. The silver ring with the dragon gleamed dully on his middle finger.

I once asked Nana why Grandpa was so quiet. What I was really asking, of course, was why he paid so little attention to me. Nana seemed to understand, her lips creasing into a tender smile. "When your grandfather was a young man," she explained, "he fought in a long war. An awful war. He saw many terrible things. Some people never recover from that kind of experience."

"Do you mean World War Two?" I asked.

She didn't nod, only repeated, "An awful war."

From the closet, I watched Grandpa pace in front of his desk. Seeming to arrive at a decision, he straightened and turned to the nearest bookcase.

"*Svelare,*" he said. Another strange word, spoken with depth and resonance.

A charge stirred the air, and the bookcase ... rippled. In the time it took for me to lean closer to the door seam, the books became other books. No more encyclopedias or insurance manuals. Humming quietly, Grandpa skipped his fingers across folios and old leather bindings. I was studying Latin in school and could translate several of the titles. Man, were they weird.

Grandpa's fingers stopped at an especially large tome, *Book of Souls*, and drew it out.

Motes of light fluttered from the spreading pages. He waved at them absently until they dissipated. Turning slowly, the book open at his chest, he traced a finger across the page, lips moving. Maybe from staring at Grandpa for so long without blinking, a purple hue took shape around him. I squeezed my eyes closed and opened them again, but the effect remained.

When a hard knock sounded, I tried to angle my view

toward the study door. Nana? But with the second bout of knocking, I realized it wasn't coming from the door. It was coming from Grandpa's steamer trunk.

Holy hell, someone's in there.

"Yes, what is it?" Grandpa answered distractedly.

Though I couldn't make out the words coming from the trunk, the voice had a sniveling quality.

"Mm-hmm," Grandpa said, still absorbed in his book.

The voice said something else.

Grandpa's finger stopped moving. The aura of light surrounding him tightened. He raised his face until his gaze lined up with mine. The book clapped closed.

My bladder jiggled again, this time in horror. When I tried to draw back, Grandpa uttered something and the coats began shoving against me. *What the...!* Through the seam in the door, I saw him swapping the book for his walking cane. My eyes jerked around, but there was nowhere to go, nowhere to hide.

All in one moment, the door opened, the coats thrust me out, his hand seized my wrist, and a steel blade flashed, biting deep into my first finger.

Ten years later

"You are fool."

I raised my eyes from the thin scar on my finger, twisting on the wooden bench to face the cart driver. For the last two hours, the Romanian man had been silent, even when I made a few stabs at conversation in Slovak. He shook the horses' dripping reins, a peasant's hat hiding the top half of a face that stared at the muddy road ahead. I'd assumed the man was reticent, not given to conversation. But had he just called me a fool?

I cleared my throat. "Come again?"

The cart's wheels jounced through another brown puddle as rain continued to patter over my hooded jacket. For miles we'd traversed nothing but fields and poor farmland, but up ahead I could make out the first houses of a village proper, weathered plaster affairs with red-tiled roofs. Perhaps in anticipation of food or rest, the pair of horses snorted and sped their clopping pace. After traveling non-stop for the last twenty-four hours, on planes, trains, and now a cart, I knew the feeling.

Just when I thought the driver had fallen back into his silence, he spoke again. "You come for curiosity."

"Sort of." I eyed him carefully—where had I heard all of this before? "I'm headed to the ruins of an old monastery. Dolhasca. Supposed to be a two-day's hike from the village. Maybe you've heard of it?"

I had managed to acquire a survey map of the area, onto which I'd plotted my best estimate of the monastery's location, but I was hoping to find someone to give me clearer directions—or better yet, to guide me.

"Why?" he asked, pronouncing it *vy?*

"Research. I'm a doctoral student. Dolhasca's founding monks are supposed to have transcribed some lost texts. I want to see if I can locate them. They may shed light on early European beliefs."

It was the same explanation I had given while applying for my research grant, but it was only half the truth. The other half was that, after years of searching, I believed I was close to locating a book that would explain who my grandfather had been, besides an insurance man.

"That is why you are fool," he said.

"And why is that, exactly?"

"The journey." He looked over to where the valley rose into dark forested hills, the white-capped Carpathian Mountains jutting beyond. "It will be your death."

I'd been warned that this region of Romania was still rife with superstition, but wow.

"Let me guess ... evil spirits?" I scoffed. The pit of hunger in my stomach, not to mention my sore butt, had lowered my tolerance for nonsense. I was going full smartass. "Ogres? Witches?"

"Wolves," he replied.

"Oh." I let out an embarrassed laugh. "Well, we have wolves too, and they're not man eaters."

"Then your wolves are not like ours."

I eyed the forest. "What makes yours so special?"

Even as I asked, a cold foreboding prickled through me. Beyond the water dripping from the brim of the man's hat, sober gray eyes fixed on mine. He palmed his sodden hat, lifted it from his head, and turned so the muted light caught his disfigured profile. The four scar lines began at his right temple—ridges through his matted black hair—and raked across his cheek. I had assumed the cloudiness of his right eye was the result of cataracts, but now I saw how the topmost scar ended at the split eyelid.

"A *wolf* did that?" I asked.

He replaced his hat. "I was young fool. I did not believe stories."

I swallowed. All right, maybe I needed to rethink my approach. "Are there any villagers who moonlight as armed escorts?"

"None will go into forest."

The cart's axles groaned as we arrived in the muddy village square. Though we were no longer in the countryside, a smell of wet beasts and turned-up earth filled the damp air. The horses clopped past a stucco church and a couple of store fronts until the driver drew back on the reins. We came to a snorting stop in front of the village's lone pension—four bedrooms with breakfast provided, if the entry in my guide-book was to be believed.

The driver climbed down and plodded around to the back of the cart. I joined him from the other side, water squelching through my hiking shoes. I eyed his battered rubber boots in envy. He threw a tarp to one side, and from between stacks of crates pulled out my traveling backpack, which he set on the steps of the pension.

I counted out several bills. "Thanks for the ride."

As he accepted the money and pressed it into a shirt pocket, I noticed the dull ring on his third finger. A familiar figure was embossed in the thick face: a rearing dragon.

"Y-your ring," I stammered. "My grandfather had one just like it. Where did you get it?"

He looked down at the ring briefly and without interest. "A street seller." Climbing back up to his seat, he took the reins in hand but hesitated mid snap. "Do not be fool," he said, peering down on me. "The journey is not for mortals. It will not forgive curiosity or covetousness. Tell your friends this."

"Friends?"

He raised his gray eyes to the pension.

"You are not only foreigner here."

3

I encountered foreigner number one just beyond the pension's entrance, in a sitting room. The young man, with a stylish tousle of blond hair and cheery blue eyes, looked to be about my age. He sat in a corner chair facing the door, a glass of dark wine in hand, as though waiting for someone to join him in drink and conversation.

"Lovely weather, eh mate?" he said in a pleasant English accent.

I wiped my shoes on the mat and dropped my pack beside the door. I was interested in food, a bath, and a bed, in that order. There was no space on my immediate itinerary for chit-chat.

"Name's James." He pushed up a sweater sleeve and crossed the room with his hand extended.

I dried my hands on the sides of my pants and accepted his hearty shake. "Everson Croft."

"Let me guess. You're also on the hunt for the fabled manuscripts of Dolhasca?"

I stopped unzipping my jacket and looked up at him.

He laughed as though we'd just shared in a particularly

clever joke. "I read the article in the *Historical Journal*, too. I'm a fifth year at Oxford. European History."

"Midtown College in New York," I replied. "Mythology."

"Sharp minds think alike, eh?" He clapped my shoulder.

"Guess so," I muttered.

He switched to an old form of Latin. *"The manuscripts are said to be in archaic Latin."*

I nodded and answered in kind. *"So I've heard."*

He beamed at me as though I'd passed some test. "Well go on," he said. "Shed your jacket, grab a towel. I'll ready you a glass of the local spirit. Not vintage, mind you, but it gets the job done."

At least he wasn't treating me like a rival. Academics could be petty that way. Take the new chairman of my history department, Professor Snodgrass. Now *there* was a piece of work. I sank into the couch and accepted the glass of wine he'd prepared. James raised his own glass brightly and we both sipped. To my surprise, the hit of alcohol, coupled with the soft cushion, soothed my travel pains and the irritability that went with them. James tugged at the white collar of a shirt that poked from his too-green sweater. He could have been a golfer taking a break from the links.

"So how long have you been here?" I asked.

"Since Monday. I was hoping to set out for the monastery yesterday, but the weather's been bloody dreadful." He sighed and gazed out a window running with rain water. Distant lightning paled his face in twin flashes.

"You sound confident in the monastery's location."

"Well, I have technology to thank for that." As he dug in his pocket, the ensuing thunder rolled in, shaking the walls. James held up what looked like a small two-way radio, a rubber antenna poking from the top. "Using a satellite map program, I was able to identify the ruins. That gave me a GPS location. According to this, the monastery is approximately 48 kilometers north by northwest from our current position." He held the device toward me. "Care to take a look?"

"No, no." I leaned away and showed my palms. "I have a way of breaking that stuff."

It was true. Technology never failed to get pissy in my presence. The last time I'd tried to use a library computer, the screen blacked out and smoke drifted from the keyboard. Seconds later, the entire college network crashed. Fortunately, I was a whiz on my mechanical typewriter.

James shrugged and returned the GPS device to his pocket.

"But, hey..." I went to retrieve my pack. "Would you mind looking over my maps and telling me if I'm in the proximity?"

"What in God's name for?" James asked. "Now that you're here, we can make the journey together."

I lowered myself back to the couch. "You wouldn't mind?"

"Two heads are better than one. I'd enjoy the company, besides."

"Well cheers to that." I raised my glass, and we drank again, my worries over the monastery's location resolved. But with the next flashes of lightning, I recalled the driver's scars, the pale ridges of tissue shining through his damp hair. The wolf's claws must have flayed the poor bastard to his skull.

"Something the matter?" James asked.

"Has anyone warned you about going into the forest?"

"Other than everyone I've talked to?" He smiled and waved a hand. "We're in the old country, mate. Good people, the very salt of the earth, but simple minds. Where there are unexplored wilds, there must be monsters, right?"

"I get your point. But I'd feel better if we had an escort. There *have* been wolf attacks."

James examined his held-up glass with an unconcerned

air. "I've already asked around. No one's interested, I'm afraid. It seems there are only four of us willing to venture into those wilds."

The driver *had* mentioned foreigners, plural. "Who are the other two?"

"Well, there's a Flor from Spain." He lowered his voice. "A treat for the eyes, but beware her tongue. I believe I still have a few welts from our little disagreement this morning at breakfast." He chuckled as he rubbed his upper arm. "The other is Bertrand, a prominent French academic. Not particularly friendly, though."

"A real United Nations," I remarked, to which James chuckled again. "And they're trying to reach Dolhasca, too?"

He nodded. "But we've all been pinned down by the weather. We have that and the monastery in common, if nothing else."

"What if we all set out together?" I asked. "The stronger our numbers, the less likely any wolves would be to mess with us, right?"

"Sounds like perfectly good reasoning to me, but you'll need to convince the others. Their interest in Dolhasca seems nothing short of *mercenary*." He pronounced the word as though the concept were far beneath him.

"Maybe we can all meet for dinner this evening," I said. "Talk it over."

"Splendid. I'll arrange it. There's a restaurant on the corner." He bussed my empty glass. "But you should go up and get some rest, my friend. You look right knackered."

I did as James suggested, finding the pension owner, an elderly woman, who showed me to a simple room on the second floor. After washing up, I lay on the single bed, the day's motion swimming through my exhausted body. It was hard to believe I was less than thirty miles from the *Book of*

Souls—a title that vanished from Grandpa's collection with his death. A title research had shown me should never have existed in the twentieth century.

But then to read of it last month in the *Historical Journal*, the author believing that Dolhasca's founding monks had transcribed reams of lost texts and tomes, among them the *Book of Souls*. I closed my eyes. To think that in two days time I could be holding the same book I had seen in Grandpa's hands ten years earlier. My thoughts began to drift on that thought.

I was nearly asleep when, in the far distance, a wolf's cry went up.

4

B ertrand shook his head emphatically, eyes closed. *"No."*

"Why not?" I asked.

"I planned a solo expedition," he replied in a stuffy French accent, "and a solo expedition it will remain."

The middle-aged man sitting across from me was tall and lean with a sour face and eyelids that fluttered when he voiced an objection, which was often. James had been right about the "not particularly friendly" bit. More to the point, he was a dick.

"And we are after the same manuscripts, no?" he continued. "Why would I want to share my findings with a group of amateurs?" He returned to his stewed rabbit with prim stabs of his fork and knife.

We had convened for dinner about an hour after I'd lain down. Thanks to the wolf howls, which had grown into a nightmare chorus, I hadn't slept a wink. Tiredness and anger now growled inside me. Before I could respond to Bertrand's "amateur" dig, James clapped his hands once.

"Well," he said cheerily. "Party of three, then?"

We all turned to Flor. With her sultry eyes, pouting lips,

and sheen of shoulder-length black hair, she was hard not to jaw-drop over. But I saw what James meant about her mercenary quality. It wasn't just in her black tank top and cargo pants, but also in the flat, almost groaning way she spoke.

"I am of the same mind as Bertrand," she said, dropping a gnawed bone onto her plate. "As much as I hate to admit it."

I looked around in exasperation. The restaurant was an older couple's home, three tables pushed into a dining room and adorned with sooty plastic flowers. In a back kitchen, pots clinked and water gurgled. Despite that we had the place to ourselves, I lowered my voice.

"Look," I said. "What I'm proposing will entail some compromise, yes. But it gives us the best chance of reaching Dolhasca. Attempt it alone and there's a chance we'll not only fail to find the monastery, but end up as wolf food."

Bertrand sniffed. "It sounds like the American is afraid."

Heat flashed over my face. "And you sound like a—"

"I asked around after our chat earlier," James interrupted. "Everson's concerns about the wolves are to be taken seriously. The history of the region is peppered with attacks on villagers, some of them fatal. Even the hunters don't dare venture into the deep forest anymore. The roaming packs have little fear of humans, it seems. And they are especially aggressive at night." Like everything else, he delivered the dire news with an almost buoyant air.

"Tales," Bertrand decided.

"And what makes you the expert?" I was struggling not to rise and smack the haughty look from his face.

He touched his napkin to his lips and took another half minute to chew and swallow. "I was educated at your Harvard University, an overpriced, overrated institution, if ever there was. I completed my doctoral work at the Sorbonne in Paris, where I have been a full professor since. My publications are extensive—perhaps you've read my tome on medieval philosophy? I have won two book awards and am presently up for a third. And I am *constantly* being asked to lecture at prestigious conferences and universities." He looked pointedly at James. "Last month I turned down an invitation from Oxford."

"Thanks for the curriculum vitae," I said, "but I missed the part where you slayed wild animals."

Bertrand went to work on his potatoes as though he hadn't heard me.

"Maybe the American is right," Flor said. "Maybe we should stick together until we reach the monastery."

I pushed my upturned palms toward her. "Thank you."

"But once there," she continued, "we will need to decide how to apportion the spoils."

Apportion? Spoils? I drew my hands back. "We're not looters, for God's sake. We're researchers." A slanting look in Flor's eyes made me hesitate. "Wait, you are a researcher, aren't you?"

"I was just testing you," Flor said. "And what I am is none of your business."

Ouch. "Well, if we're going to join forces, I think James and I need to know what you're doing here."

"Good luck, my friend." James chuckled. "Flor and I have danced around the question a few times this week, haven't we, love?"

Flor narrowed her eyes at him.

I decided not to press her, lest she change her mind about joining our party. Sharp-tongued or not, I didn't like the thought of her attempting the journey alone. Plus, her presence strengthened our numbers.

"All right," I said. "So that's three. Bertrand? Last chance."

He snorted and pushed himself back from his half-finished plate. "I would just as soon join the Three Stooges." He slapped a pair of bills on the table and, donning his slicker and rain hat, strode from the restaurant. It wasn't until he was gone that I saw he had underpaid.

James looked from the closing door to Flor and me. "So," he said with a happy sigh. "What time shall we be off?"

"The weather is scheduled to improve around noon tomorrow," Flor said. "We should reach the monastery late the following day. If you two do not slow me down."

I slid James a sidelong smirk. "Yeah, we'll try to keep up."

He grinned back. "Well, I do like the sound of only spending one night in the forest each way."

"And I have an idea for some wolf repellent," I said.

5

F lor came down to the breakfast table the next morning as James and I were finishing up. Her grunted response to our greetings suggested she wasn't a morning person. That didn't stop her stray hair and sleepy face from playing games with my imagination though. I coughed into a fist.

"The Frenchman is gone," she stated, ripping a chunk of bread from the loaf and slathering it with butter.

"Gone for a walk?" I asked. "Or *gone* gone."

"He has taken everything with him." The chunk disappeared into her mouth, and she chewed morosely.

"I heard him moving about early this morning," James said. "It seems he's set out on his own, the poor sod."

"Yeah, to beat us there," I grumbled. "Let's just hope we don't arrive to a fortified monastery." Though I wouldn't have put something like that past Bertrand, concern for his safety moved through me. I reminded myself that we had warned him, that he was a grown man.

As for *our* safety...

"If you'll excuse me," I said, standing from the table. "The pension owner gave me kitchen privileges for the next hour, and there's something I need to cook."

"Then it looks like I'll have this lovely fount of conversation all to myself," James said, cutting his sparkling eyes to Flor. She stopped chewing long enough to glower at him.

Geez. Even *that* look on her was amazing.

I stumbled into a chair as I left the room.

SINCE I WAS A YOUNG BOY, MY HEAD BARELY AS HIGH AS NANA'S hip, cooking had fascinated me. Combining disparate ingredients. Getting the proportions just right. Adding energy in the form of heat. All to end up with something whose whole was greater—or at least tastier—than the sum of its parts. And Nana's meals were some of the tastiest I'd ever had.

That process, that *alchemy* I suppose you could call it, still impressed me.

I placed a cast-iron pot of water onto the gas stove. From the refrigerator, I pulled out a large bag of Romanian hot peppers I'd picked up at the local grocer. I pounded the pale-green peppers with the flat side of a butcher knife, releasing the juice and seeds, and scraped the mess into the pot. Finding the pension's black pepper, I ground it liberally into the steaming mixture.

James arrived twenty minutes later, as I was funneling the final dregs of the pepper spray between three spray bottles.

"Ah, your wolf repellent, I presume?"

"I made it extra strong, so be extra careful." I screwed on the plastic nozzles and handed him a bottle. "It so much as touches your skin, you'll think you're under a fire-ant attack, so you definitely don't want to get any in your eyes. A wolf's eyes are fine."

Flor appeared from behind James and claimed her bottle. She smirked as she wrapped her fingers around the plastic trigger. "They are cute," she remarked.

"Cute?" I'd been hoping for badass. "Just watch where you point it."

Her lips straightened as she lowered the bottle to her side. "We need to set out."

"But it's still dreadful," James said, lowering his head to the window to be sure.

Flor's dark eyes fixed on mine. "What you said about Bertrand wanting to reach the monastery before us. It disturbs me."

"Why?" I asked.

She peered over a shoulder, as though the man might be standing behind her, and then stepped close enough for me to feel her heat.

"Because he is not who he claims to be."

———

WE SET OUT AN HOUR LATER, TROMPING UP A MUDDY ROAD that led from the village into the foothills. Families paused in their field work to stare at us through the gray rain, their wan faces impossible to read. At a final farmhouse, I caught an elderly woman making the sign of the cross before withdrawing from her dark window and closing the shutters.

Okay. That wasn't creepy or anything.

I jogged every few paces to keep up with Flor, and I noticed James doing the same. In her black combat boots, she seemed intent on taking the forest by bloody conquest. In addition to her backpack, she had set out with a titanium suitcase, declining James's and my offers to carry it for her.

When we'd asked what was inside, she had given the one-word answer, "Equipment."

"So," I breathed, when I'd pulled even with her again. "Are you going to tell us about Bertrand now, or what?"

"He is a fraud," she said.

"Really? In what way?"

"What he told you last night?" She lowered her eyelids to half mast and affected a French accent. "'I am star professor. I am coveted speaker. I am genius.' It is all bullshit."

James laughed. "Not bad. And how did you discover that delightful gem?"

"Google," she said.

"Google?" I peered back down toward the remote village. "Was there an internet cafe I missed?"

"I have a satellite phone. I had someone look into his claims."

"Well," James said. "A spy after my own heart."

Flor ignored the comment, which gave me private pleasure. While James and I might not have been academic rivals, I sensed a growing competition between us for Flor's attention. A competition I was determined to win. "Bertrand teaches in Paris," she said. "But at what they call a *primaire*."

"Wait," I said. "He's an *elementary school* teacher?"

"So, his talk about Harvard and the Sorbonne?" James chimed in. "The book awards?"

"His only publication is a personal web page," Flor replied. "Pure drivel."

I snorted, unable to believe the man's audacity. So what was he doing here? Trying to garner recognition? To become the academic celebrity he'd already invented for himself?

"Wow," I remarked, "and he had the nerve to call *us* amateurs."

"That settles that, I suppose," James said. "But what about us, love?"

Flor's face whipped toward him. "What about you?"

"Well, surely you didn't stop with our good man Bertrand."

It took me a moment to understand what James was suggesting. Flor had her contact look into us as well.

"Do not worry," she snapped. "Your stories check out. So far."

And yours? I wanted to ask. But the road narrowed suddenly, the encroaching trees pressing us into a single file. Flor took the lead while I fell to the rear. Almost immediately, the temperature dropped several degrees, and the air thickened with humidity. A strange fatigue overcame me. But while I labored with each step, the other two marched ahead.

"Hey, American," Flor called through the foliage. "Move your ass. We have many kilometers to cover."

James turned around and tipped me a wink.

6

The first wolf call arrived late that afternoon, a long, chilling cry.

Flor and James stopped to listen, allowing me time to catch up. I stood on shaky legs, searching the seams in the trees. The forest we were ascending through had grown darker and more knotted with each mile until it looked like something out of a Grimm's fairytale. My gaze darted toward the sound of a snapping branch. I thought I caught a figure duck behind a black tree, but the forest had been playing tricks on my eyes all afternoon.

"Sounded like quite a big one," James said of the cry. "Assertive, too."

"Yes, but it is far away," Flor said. "Kilometers. We need to keep going. Bertrand had a four-hour head start."

James consulted his GPS device. "We're making decent time, in any case."

"It could be better," Flor remarked, glancing over at me.

Her shirt hiked up as she turned, and I caught myself gawking at a glistening show of skin above her right hip. I was going on six months since my last girlfriend kicked me to the curb, and the yearning for that kind of companionship was starting to feel like a clinical condition. Maybe when I returned to New York I'd look into getting a cat. Something uncomplicated.

"How you holding up, mate?" James asked, slowing to match my pace.

"Fine." In fact, I was exhausted. "Hey, you've been talking to her most of the day," I said in a lowered voice and with a shot of envy. "Any insights into her motive for wanting to go to the monastery? Or why she's so hell bent on getting there ahead of Bertrand?"

"I'm afraid not. And if you intend on taking up the question with her again, I advise you to step carefully. She's a bit of a minefield, that one."

"So I've noticed." My gaze locked onto the titanium case swinging from her arm.

Before I could wonder aloud about its contents, James said, "The folklore in these parts should interest someone in your line of study. Did you know they have a version of a werewolf called a *pricolici*?"

I ventured a glance at the dark forest behind us. "Is now really the best time?"

"Ooh, dreadful creatures," he went on. "Fast, powerful, smart as humans, but nigh impossible to kill. And they don't abide by the moon cycles as far as their wolf forms go. That's a constant condition. As far as their temperaments?" He gave a knowing laugh. "The waxing moon is supposed to make them more blood thirsty. And I do believe we're coming on a full moon this week."

When another cycle of howling started, James's eyes gleamed as though the wolves had just made his point for him.

"Thanks for that info," I muttered.

While James trotted to catch up to Flor, I glanced around again, my anxiety needle trembling in the orange. Not that I believed in werewolves, or needed to—actual wolves were worrying enough. Then again, if magic could exist in our world, why not monsters? Because whatever I had witnessed from my grandfather's closet that night had looked an awful lot like magic.

Magic I wasn't supposed to have seen.

I stared at Grandpa's face, shock icing over my own. His hazel-blue eyes studied the blood welling from my finger, the lines around his mouth turning down. One hand clamped my wrist, but I was more concerned by his other hand. The one gripping a sword that, only seconds before, had been his walking cane. A sword he had just drawn across my finger faster than I could blink.

The wound began to sting, then burn, pulling a murmur from my lips.

His eyes snapped to mine. Hard Germanic eyes. "You should not hide up here."

With those thick, accented words, the attic room seemed to take form again, everything returning from some gray haze. The antique desk, the crowded bookshelves, the old steamer trunk. Though I couldn't see the closet I had been crouched inside, I could smell the stuffy coats behind me.

"How did you get in?" he demanded.

"Wh-what?"

"How did you enter my room?"

My gaze shifted to the door. No latching system. Not even a keyhole to peek through. But always locked. Through the dense wood, I had often picked up vibrations of muffled words, liturgical-like chants, and once, a high, chilling voice that sounded like nothing I'd ever heard. The voice gave me nightmares for a month. But it didn't keep me from coming back to listen.

"I-I opened the door."

"How?"

The word. There was a strange word Grandpa would utter every time he stood outside his attic door before he turned the knob. As though he were muttering a brusque greeting to someone.

"I said what you say."

His grip tightened on my wrist as he leaned closer. "And what do I say?"

"*Apri—*" I cleared my throat. "*Aprire.*"

As had happened when I'd spoken the word earlier, a current passed through me, and a pressure in the room seemed to release, like when your ears popped after an airplane flight. Grandpa blinked twice. He peered at the door for a full minute, then closed his eyes and exhaled through his large nostrils, as though he had just arrived at a grave conclusion.

"You should not hide up here," he repeated, releasing my wrist and straightening. "You should not even be in here. Ever."

I pulled my hand toward my chest, wounded finger extended, tears standing in my eyes. "Okay."

I flinched when he reached down, but it was only to wipe the blood away with his large thumb. He uttered something as he ran the blood-smeared thumb up and down the flat of the sword before sliding it back into the cane. He strode to the door, his dark linen suit stiff on his tall frame.

I followed, casting wary glances at the trunk, silent now,

and the bookshelves that held encyclopedias and reference books once more. Had I imagined everything?

"You are curious," Grandpa said as he opened the door for me. "But you must not be foolish. Things heard cannot be unheard. Things seen unseen. Things spoken unspoken. And it is this last that is most important for those of our blood."

"Yes, sir," I said, not knowing what in the hell he was talking about.

He stared at me sternly for another moment, then dismissed me with a nod.

I pattered down the narrow staircase, scared and confused. I had been in Nana and Grandpa's care ever since my mother had died, which was ever since I could remember, and neither had ever hurt me. And on my birthday?

Arriving in my room, I closed the door behind me with a foot, blind to the opened presents spread over my bed. *He sliced my finger,* I thought. I was afraid to look, already anticipating the flayed fat pad, maybe even a bloody knot of bone. The slice had felt that deep.

But when I looked down, all I saw was a faint white line.

7

T he wolf calls grew in number with the fading light. They volleyed back and forth, as though several had picked up our scent and were telling the others. When an especially loud cry rent the air, I jogged to catch up to James and Flor.

"I say we make camp," I blurted. "Build a nice fire, set up some kind of watch." My heart beat hard in my chest as I pointed off to the right. "There's a flat spot over there, plenty of fallen limbs."

James nodded his approval, then turned to Flor.

She looked at her watch and sighed. "Fine."

I went to work on the fire while James and Flor set up their tents. Using hand sanitizer as starter fuel, I got a decent-sized blaze going before dusk became full dark. After gathering up a reserve of limbs to last the night, the three of us ate our dinners around the fire. I noticed Flor didn't have my homemade repellent at hand.

"Where's your bottle?" I asked.

"I left it at the pension."

"On purpose?"

"The wolves will not come close to the fire."

Deeper in the forest, above her right shoulder, a golden pair of eyes flashed and disappeared. And they weren't the only ones. More sets of eyes winked in and out of the trees, like coins from a dark well. "Better rethink that logic," I said, "because they're already here."

I shot to my feet, fingers wrapping the trigger of my spray bottle—which suddenly felt puny to the task. James rose with his bottle as well, but more in curiosity than fear, it seemed.

Flor remained seated. "That is as close as they will come."

"Don't know about that, love," James said. "At least one of them sounds determined to make a fireside appearance."

I turned to where James was aiming his bottle, away from the flashing of eyes. Then I heard it too: the sound of something large running through wet leaves, coming straight for us. A moment later, a shadow broke into the light.

Squinting, I rapid-fired the plastic trigger.

Shouts went up. Too late, I saw the figure wasn't a wolf, but a person. The aerosol of pepper spray that enveloped the man sent him shrieking to the ground, hands to his eyes. I noted the hair flapping from his slipping hood, and then the lumpy pack on the man's back.

"My God, is that Bertrand?" James asked.

If there was any doubt, his stuffy voice removed it. "You animals!" Bertrand cried. "What kind of poison have you put into my eyes?"

"Just stop rubbing them," I said with the annoyance of someone who's just had the crap needlessly scared from him. I hurried to my pack and returned with a bottle of milk, which I'd stowed in the event of an accident.

"What are you doing?" Bertrand sputtered, as the milk splashed over his face.

"Neutralizing the pepper, you idiot. Now hold still and let it flush everything out."

He stopped slapping and writhing long enough to blink the milk into his bloodshot eyes.

"There," I said, recapping the bottle with a sigh. "Give it a few seconds."

James offered him a handkerchief, which Bertrand snatched away and used to mop his face and then pinch into the corners of his eyes. I noticed Flor had remained on her side of the fire the whole time, a smile slanting her lips. My face flushed as I imagined how slap-sticky we must have looked. But the commotion must also have scared the wolves away, because I could no longer see their eyes.

I turned back to Bertrand, who was pushing himself to his knees.

"Correct me if I'm wrong," I said, "but was that you fleeing for your life?" I was still bristling over the American-is-afraid jab. Not to mention his whole intellectual façade. "It couldn't have had anything to do with those wolf *tales*, as you called them last night, could it?"

"Don't be preposterous," he replied stiffly, gaining his feet. "I was preparing my own camp over there when I saw your fire. It made no sense to pass the night alone, so I decided to join you."

"Which involved running here at full speed."

"Walk? Run? What does it matter how I arrived?" he spat. "Though I am beginning to see my mistake."

I studied his black slicker and lined it up with the shadows I'd glimpsed earlier, the snapping of branches, the feeling of being watched. "How long have you been following us?"

He blinked and straightened. "How *dare* you suggest—"

"Oh, spare us the dramatics," I said. "That's why you set

out early, isn't it? Not to get a head start, but to hide until we'd passed and then tail us. You don't know the precise location of the monastery. Your plan was to let us lead you there and then run ahead and claim the discovery and anything inside for yourself. It was all going along just hunky-dory until the wolves turned up. And then your little scheme didn't seem so cunning, did it?"

"You have been watching too many stupid American movies," he muttered, even as he shot nervous glances into the forest.

"Very good," James said, stepping between us. "The important thing is that we're all safe. Now, how should we divide up the shifts?"

"After all this excitement, you boys need your rest," Flor said. "I will take the first."

"And I the second," Bertrand announced. "Which leaves you to take the third, and you the fourth." He pointed to me and James in turn, as though we were his teaching assistants.

"Can you believe this guy?" I said, anger climbing my neck. "You're not even a prof—"

"That will work just fine," James interrupted. After Bertrand had given a self-satisfied nod and begun unpacking his shelter, James guided me a few steps away. "Better he doesn't know we're onto him, hmm?"

I narrowed my eyes at Bertrand. I had never been able to stand officious jerks, especially lying ones.

"And why's that?" I asked.

"Well, if he suspects we know his true story, he's likely to behave more carefully, cover his tracks. Then we may never learn what he's doing here. We keep a sly eye on him, and sooner or later he'll slip up."

I nodded reluctantly. "And Flor?"

"Oh, she's on board. We had the same chat earlier."

"No, I mean, shouldn't we be keeping an eye on her, as well?"

"Why, you're quite right," James said.

I noticed that ever since we'd arrived at the campsite, her titanium case had never been more than an arm's length away from her. I nodded at it now. "I'll use my shift to see if I can get a peek at whatever's she's carrying. Maybe it'll tip us off to what she's doing here."

"Careful, mate," he said. "Minefield, remember?"

"Yeah, I'm used to those."

8

I was awakened by muttered curses and red light against my eyelids, growing brighter. I had fallen asleep to a modest campfire, an ample reserve of wood stacked beside it. Now I squinted my eyes open to a furious blaze. One onto which Bertrand was dumping the final thick branches.

"What in the hell are you doing?" I hissed, kicking away my sleeping bag and unzipping my fly net. "You're using up all the fuel!"

Bertrand acknowledged me with a tight glance before wiping off his hands and sweeping his gaze over the forest. When I focused past him, all the fight fell out of me. The wolves were back and crowding against the boundary between firelight and darkness, flashing eyes set in long, gray faces. There were more of them than earlier, and whether it was some trick of light, they looked like small bulls.

"They were closer before I fed the blaze," Bertrand said.

"That's genius, professor, but we're out of wood now."

I scanned our campsite, but we had cleared it of branches. The only fuel lay beyond the ring of predators, who watched silently. No more pack to call. They were all here.

I flinched when the fire snapped behind me and stove in slightly. As the orb of light shrank, the wolves inched nearer. The closest ones were only thirty feet away.

"Everyone up!" I called, rustling James's tent and Flor's tarp. "We've got company."

James emerged first and looked around sleepily. "Well, I'd say."

"Get your repellent," I told him.

"I do applaud your ingenuity," he said, arriving beside me. He peered from our bottles back to the wolves. "However, it looks as if the current advantage lies with our furry friends."

I shook my bottle to stir up the pepper dregs. "You saw what this stuff did to the professor. It doesn't take much. I say we release a few sprays into the wind, enough to warn them away."

"Or more likely provoke them into an attack," Bertrand said from behind us.

"Funny coming from a man who said they were harmless," I growled.

James turned to me. "Bertrand does make a case."

I checked my watch and did the math. "The sun doesn't come up for another five hours. Our fire, whose exhaustion the brilliant professor here saw fit to hasten, isn't going to last another two."

The fire stove in again, and the wolves inched forward a foot. Several snapped at one another for position, fangs bright and lethal in the firelight.

"Hmm," James said. "I see your point."

We raised our spray bottles.

"Don't," Bertrand warned, his voice as taut as a guy wire. "They will attack."

"Three squirts," I said to James. "You fan yours out a little that way. I'll aim a little more this way."

"Got it."

"On my countdown," I said, my hand trembling. "Three... two..."

"No!" Bertrand leapt between us and brought his fist down on my forearm. The bottle fell to the ground. James's grunt told me Bertrand had struck him as well. "I will not be a victim of your stupidity!"

He kicked my bottle away and wrestled with James for his.

I turned to where the bottle rolled to a stop, on the verge of the firelight. One of the wolves leaned forward to sniff it. Was it a wolf? Its snout seemed too thick, too blunt, teeth hooking over its lower jaw. And its front paw splayed out like a bear's instead of a canine's, ending in large claws. No wonder the driver's scars had looked like the work of a grizzly. James's account of the Romanian werewolf, the *pricolici,* flashed through my mind.

The beast bared its fangs at the bottle, then up at me, as though assigning blame for the poison, before drawing back into the shadows again.

Behind me, James spoke through clenched teeth, "You're going about this rather roughly."

I looked to find him and Bertrand still grappling for the bottle. The barks and snarls from the ring of wolves rose in pitch. I hooked an arm around Bertrand's throat and tried to pull him away.

"Stop fighting, *goddammit,*" I hissed in his ear. "You're exciting them."

"You are the ones ... exciting them," Bertrand grunted, pistoning a sharp elbow into my ribs.

A single ragged cry went up and I felt, more than heard, the circle of wolves collapse. I released Bertrand and turned in time to meet the beast plowing into me. Two hundred pounds of brawn and thick, wet hair drove me onto my back, foul breath breaking against my face. The beast strained against my forearm, which I'd managed to brace against its throat. Lips drew from a double set of fanged teeth as its dense brow collapsed over furious eyes. Eyes that, save for their deep yellow irises, appeared almost human.

I was struggling against its straining neck, and losing, when a tight explosion pierced the tumult.

Something hot sprayed my face. The wolf on top of me crashed to its side and then tore at the ground to right itself. More explosions sounded, and the wolves fled, one dragging a blood-drenched hind leg.

I thrashed to my feet, looking from the disappearing wolves to the source of the explosions. Across the fire, Flor stood holding what looked like a military-grade rifle. She scanned the woods in a three-hundred-sixty-degree arc, smoke drifting from the barrel. When she faced me once more, she said, "You wanted to know what was in the case?"

My shocked gaze fell to the open titanium container at her feet, the black foam bed inside designed to hold the disassembled rifle.

"Wow," I said, wiping wolf blood from my face. "Good planning."

I turned to find James climbing from the ground, excitement coloring his pink cheeks. Bertrand, who had fallen to his back nearby, continued to slap the air as though the wolves were still attacking.

"Are either of you injured?" I asked.

James gave his spray bottle a light toss. "Your repellent worked a charm, my friend," he said, catching it again. "Got two right in the old peepers before Flor here came to the rescue."

"Bertrand?" I asked, stooping beside him.

He had stopped thrashing and was grasping his ankle in both hands now. Blood glistened between his fingers. "I told you not to excite them," he hissed through his crooked teeth. "Why didn't you imbeciles listen? And my food bag! They have taken my food bag!"

I shoved down my annoyance and made him move his hands. The gash was bad, but more worrying was the swelling. One of the wolves had gotten its jaws around him pretty good. I raised my face to James and Flor. "Ankle looks ugly. Could be broken. Should we draw straws to see who takes him back?"

"I cannot," Flor said, not bothering to elaborate.

James rubbed his neck. "And I'm afraid this is my one crack to graduate."

I leaned my hands against my thighs and sighed. I could ask James to locate the *Book of Souls*, transcribe as much as he could, and mail the notes to me back in the States. I would compensate him, of course. But man, to be this close...

"All right," I said to Bertrand. "Looks like it's you and me. We'll head down in the morning."

He shoved me away. "Nonsense! I will not go back and have these two ruin what may be the most important finding of our lifetimes." He struggled to his knees, then to one foot. But when he attempted to step with his injured leg, he screamed and fell to the ground again.

"Would you look at yourself?" I said. "You can't even walk."

"It is only a sprain. Splint it and you will see. Tomorrow, I will be ready to travel."

"Your bag's gone," I reminded him. "You have no food."

Grunting, Bertrand crawled on hands and knees to his tent, zipping it closed behind him.

"Just what we need," I muttered. "Dead weight."

"Well," James said cheerily. "Shall we gather some more wood, then get a little shut eye before we're off again?"

"I will take the remaining shifts," Flor declared, rifle propped over her shoulder.

Neither James nor I argued.

9

W e set out the next morning, Bertrand cursing with every hopping step. We had fashioned a splint for him using cut-up sections of my backpack's interior frame and some sports tape Flor happened to be carrying.

"You doing all right?" I called back to him.

"Do not worry about me," he snapped, leaning on his branches-cum-crutches. "I know the way."

Sure you do, prof.

I imagined the injury had thrown a wrench into whatever he'd been planning. On the flip side, the injury meant one less worry for the rest of us. Far easier to keep tabs on a crippled fraud than an able-bodied one.

Late in the afternoon, James signaled to us. "It should be just over the pass."

Thank God. The dread of camping in the forest again had been building like a migraine. There was still the return journey to the village, but I'd worry about that in a few days.

Behind me, I could hear Bertrand grunting to catch up, probably hoping to overtake us, but James and Flor were too far ahead. Before long, their voices rose in excitement. When

I arrived at the mountain pass, I saw why. Where the trees began to thin, a sizeable stone structure took shape against a cliff face. Exhilaration surged through me.

Dolhasca, the forgotten monastery.

"Wait!" Bertrand called after us. "We should enter by seniority!"

I ignored him and picked my way down toward the others. The large monastery had been built like a fortress, tall stone walls with a crenellated tower at one corner. The rear of the building ended at the cliff face, as though the mountain had sheared it in half.

"Seems we aren't the first ones here," James said when I arrived beside him.

He was examining a doorway that looked to have been bricked over but later broken down, toppled stones cast to one side. I tilted a nearby stone with a shoe, revealing a deep pocket of earth underneath.

"This happened a while ago," I said.

"Looters," Flor announced, in what sounded like disdain. "They are everywhere."

"Well, let's just hope they left the manuscripts alone."

"You don't sound very optimistic," James said.

"Because I'm not." I donned my headlamp. "The manuscripts would have been worth a fortune on the black market." And if they *had* been sold on the black market, I could kiss the *Book of Souls* goodbye. I would never be able to track it down in the dark network of buyers and sellers.

Flor stepped forward. "I wonder if they are the same ones who wrote this." I followed her squinting gaze to a message scrawled beside the door in what looked like charcoal. *"Prekliaty."*

"It's the Slovak word for *cursed*," I said.

"A warning?" James frowned. "Seems odd for looters to leave a public service announcement."

"Or maybe the message was intended to keep looters away," I said. "As a scare tactic." I looked from the message back to the busted-up stones. "Though a lot of good it did."

"Enough talk." Flor snapped on a headlamp and stepped through the opening.

"Wait," came Bertrand's voice, his head appearing above the pass. "I don't have a light!"

James filed in after Flor, and I took up the rear. We soon found ourselves on a covered walk that framed a stone-riddled courtyard. The open space had probably been a garden at one time, and it wasn't hard to imagine robed monks strolling along its paths.

"Let's split up," I said, peering down the covered walk to our right and left, picking out the shadows of doorways. "We can take a quick inventory of what's here before Bertrand arrives."

James nodded. "I'll search the tower, if you and Flor want to begin down here."

"Sounds like a plan," I said. "And Flor, we're just looking right now. Not taking, okay?"

"Bite me," she snapped and marched away.

"Well, good luck everyone," James said merrily before departing.

I set off in the opposite direction as Flor, my ego smarting from her parting words. What was it about me that put women off? My sarcasm? My face? As I shone my light over-head, the questions dissolved from my thoughts. Though the monastery had appeared forbidding from the outside, hand-some stonework adorned the interior, including the walk-way's vaulted ceiling. Romanesque pillars stood every fifteen feet or so, though several had toppled.

Not a bad place to hang out for a few days.

I shot my beam into doorways, illuminating what looked to have been prayer cells and former dormitories, all empty now save for scattered rubble and fallen timber beams. In the wall opposite the one we'd entered through, an arched doorway opened into the cliff face. From either the chill air or my own foreboding, my arms broke out in fleshy bumps.

I ducked into the doorway and soon emerged into a room at the far end of a corridor. My beam found a gruesome monster's face. Stifling a yell, I swung the beam over and hit the creature's twin. I staggered backwards, nearly falling.

I hesitated, my heart slamming—and then let out a shaky laugh.

Gargoyles.

I walked up to the devilish works of stone, the pair crouched on pedestals that flanked a descending staircase. The details were impressive, down to the fangs that extended to the gargoyle's knobby knees. The statues seemed at odds with the rest of the monastery, but I was more concerned about the staircase. My headlamp wavered into the deep darkness.

As much as I hated the word, I had a *phobia* of being underground, a condition that made it feel as if someone was sitting on my chest. Already, I was struggling to inhale a full breath.

I was debating whether to descend when, on a lintel above the steps, I caught sight of a chiseled word:

SCRIPTORIUM

The library!

In my excitement, I almost called for James before realizing I couldn't do so without alerting Flor. Bertrand, too, if he had made it inside by now. Still not knowing their designs on the texts, I couldn't take any chances—especially with Flor bearing a high-powered rifle.

Her echoing voice sounded from the courtyard. "Everson? Where are you?"

Before my phobia could gain the upper hand, I hurried down the steps, through cold currents of air and a growing odor of what smelled like garbage. I was almost to the bottom when my beam illuminated the smell's source. Two bodies stretched across the stairs while a third rested on the library floor, face up. Flashlight parts lay scattered, broken plastic glinting around metal tubes.

I clapped a hand over my mouth and braced myself against the wall. They were the first corpses I had ever seen. When my heart settled, I stole up to the closer bodies. Faded clothing draped what remained of them, their dried skin vacuum-sealed to bone, skulls wispy with hair. From up the stairwell, footfalls echoed, and a pair of lights swelled into view.

"Down here," I wheezed.

JAMES SQUATTED BESIDE THE BODY ON THE LIBRARY FLOOR, LIPS frowning. "Bruising over the face and torso, like the others. Broken limbs. Crushed skull." He pinched a faded red sleeve. "Judging by the attire, I'd say gypsies."

"And look at this." My headlamp illuminated a black dagger with a shattered blade.

"Looters," Flor decided for the second time that afternoon. "I found a room with their things. Bedding, pickaxes, backpacks."

"Anything in the packs?" I asked hopefully.

"Just clothes and extra batteries, some rotten food."

I felt my optimism crumple into a wad as I worked out what had likely happened. "Someone in their party must have murdered the other three and then made off with the loot. Probably the manuscripts, given that it occurred down here." I eyed the rifle slung across Flor's back, wondering if that had been *her* intention. She seemed to know a lot about looting.

"No. There is bedding for four upstairs," she said. "And there are still four bags."

James stood and shone his light around. "Suggesting there must be a fourth body somewhere."

"Or the fourth person fled," I suggested.

"Fled what?" Flor snapped.

I was thinking of the scrawled message outside the front door—*cursed*—almost certain now the fourth looter had left it after fleeing whatever had killed his companions. But I didn't say anything.

"Well, we're here," James pointed out with a smile. "What say we have a look about?"

The library was just large enough for us to spread apart while keeping an eye on one another, which we all seemed to be doing. Though whether for each other's safety or from suspicion, I couldn't tell. Probably both. Pillars and empty shelves loomed in and out of view. I toed through the dust on the floor, turning up small brass nails and, in a far corner, a leather cover.

The three of us met in the rear of the room where an archway stood over another stairwell. James was leaning toward a stone in the wall beside the opening, running a finger over a faint engraving.

"Vault of forbidden texts," I translated from Latin.

"This is it," Flor declared. She started down, James and I following closely.

"It's funny, mate," James whispered to me. "If the texts are forbidden, I would have expected a thick door, a hidden wall, something to keep people from nosing about. But there were no signs the stairwell had been broken into."

I nodded. That was bothering me too. We arrived in a lower chamber, passing through what felt like a chilly curtain of energy. Our lights sliced around a cylindrical room the size of a gazebo. Deep shelves had been cut into the stone wall— all of them empty.

"*Mierda,*" Flor cursed.

"This *is* a disappointment," James agreed.

Disappointment? My heart felt as though it had been pulled from my chest and set adrift. With no living family to speak of, the *Book of Souls* was to have been my line to Grandpa, to who he was. Not the bull about him working in insurance, but who he had *really* been. Why he spoke in unusual tongues. Why strange forces held his door closed. Why things in his room talked and changed. And why, on the night he had caught me in his study, he had spoken with such gravity about the responsibilities of "those of our blood."

"Do you hear that?" Flor asked.

James and I followed her dark gaze to the ceiling. A moment later, I heard it too. Clunking footsteps, crossing the floor of the main library. Too heavy to be Bertrand's.

I swallowed dryly. "Were either of you expecting company?"

10

F lor signaled for us to kill our lights. When we did, a coal-black darkness collapsed against us. In the absence of sight, my hearing sharpened. I could make out Flor's and James's shallow breaths, and one floor up, those heavy footfalls, coming nearer.

Two sets of them.

Fabric whispered—Flor sliding her rifle around to her front. "We are too vulnerable down here," she whispered. "We need to go up, see who it is."

I felt Flor edge past me, her foot scuffing lightly onto the bottom step. I swam an arm after her until my hand met the stairwell's cold wall. I ascended slowly, aware of Flor's progress ahead and James's behind, glad as hell we had all come together.

But who were we dealing with? Fellow researchers? More looters?

Not realizing the stairs had ended, I stepped awkwardly and stumbled against Flor's back. Holding her taut shoulders, I stared around the darkness as James bumped up beside me. I had expected to see flashlight beams or candles out ahead of us, but I couldn't even hear the footsteps anymore.

"One o'clock," Flor whispered.

I released her shoulders and listened. "I don't hear anything."

"Fingers on your light switches." Flor's quiet voice hummed with tension. "Now!"

Our lights blew open the darkness at the same time. And there they were—the frigging gargoyles from upstairs. With the sound of grinding stone, their heads swiveled toward us.

"Mother f—"

Explosions from Flor's rifle obliterated the rest of my mind-blown expletive. Sparks flew from the charging monstrosities and bullets caromed, one whining past my head. But I couldn't move.

"Spread out!" Flor called.

With the gargoyles almost on top of us, something kick-started in my brain. I took off to the left, weaving around pillars, my headlamp jostling madly. *Okay, this makes no sense. No flipping sense whatsoever.* When I turned to check on the others, one of the gargoyles rose over me.

I threw myself from the path of its descending fist and landed in an awkward roll, clunking several times over my backpack. The gargoyle's fist cracked into stone behind me, shaking the library's foundation.

Perhaps for my academic background, I had a bad habit of trying to make sense of situations that required a pure fight-or-flight response. But as I scrabbled to my feet, my mind was connecting the curtain of energy in the vault to the *cursed* warning to the bludgeoned looters. Had our presence downstairs triggered some sort of alarm? One that animated the gargoyles? I had seen some strange stuff in Grandpa's study, but this was taking it to a whole new level.

I stumbled backwards, my light swimming over the advancing gargoyle. Beyond the creature, Flor's and James's own lights lashed around. Rifle bursts collided with shouting, but I couldn't tell how my travel companions were faring.

Something rammed my back hard enough to rattle my teeth. I pawed to both sides to find I had not only backed into a wall, but a corner. The gargoyle stalked toward me, spreading its arms to prevent my escape.

"Hey, can we talk about this?" I stammered.

The gargoyle reached down and grasped my head like a basketball. The crushing pressure registered as bright lights behind my eyes. I didn't know what kind of pounds per square inch we were talking, but it had to be testing my skull's limits. Grasping the gargoyle's wrist in both hands, I pulled myself up and kicked. Its stone stomach stopped my heel cold. The gargoyle responded with a knee that collapsed my own belly. Then it flung me away.

I wrapped my head with my arms, sure I was going to splat into a pillar. Instead, I hit the ground pack-first and flopped onto my stomach. I lay stunned. Unable to move or breathe. The rifle bursts had stopped, and I couldn't hear Flor or James. Just the gargoyle, its stone steps cracking toward me.

You're not exciting enough, my last girlfriend had said. *All you ever do is read,* she'd said.

I winced and raised my face, the weak headlamp finding the creature's knees. Beyond, I glimpsed one of the battered and dried-out corpses on the steps. God, I didn't want to end up like those guys. I lifted my light to the gargoyle's horned snout and narrow chiseled eyes. I didn't suppose it would do any good to explain I was a researcher and not a looter.

The gargoyle arrived in front of me and drew back a leg.

"Hey..." I rasped, holding an arm out. "Easy there..."

Its stone lips trembled from snarling teeth. I curled into a ball, anticipating the impact of the organ-crushing kick.

Only it didn't arrive. After another second, I peeked between my forearms. The gargoyle was frozen in place, balanced on one leg. Then, very slowly, it began to tip to the side. Its eventual collision with the floor snapped an arm at the elbow and shattered both fangs.

I scrambled to my feet, expecting the gargoyle to rise again and resume its attack, but whatever force had possessed it moments before seemed to have broken apart like the statue.

"Well," James said, appearing from behind a pillar, "maybe not as skilled a toss as your cowboys, but it seems I lassoed the bugger all the same." I had no idea what he was talking about until he crouched and fingered something around the gargoyle's neck.

I took a tentative step closer. "What is that?"

"A rock salt necklace," he replied. "Before you arrived in town, a villager talked Flor and me into buying a pair. Claimed it would dispel evil magic. They didn't seem to be doing much in our packs, so I got the idea to throw one around his partner over there. I'll be damned if it didn't work."

I turned my head to where, across the room, Flor's light illuminated the other gargoyle, also toppled.

James clapped my shoulder. "Seems I got to yours just in time."

"No kidding," I said. "Thanks."

"The American is okay?" Flor asked, striding up to us.

"I'll live." When I coughed, pain stabbed through my ribs. I nodded at a spot on her upper arm slick with blood. "What about you?"

She shrugged it off. "A bullet graze."

I turned to James. "And you?"

"Took a slight knock to the head. Nothing a little whiskey can't cure."

"Good, because we have work to do." Maybe it was pain endorphins, but my various injuries seemed to be having a sedating, focusing effect. Manuscripts or not, we still had to survive the night. "Three things, specifically. Number one, we need to block the front door. I don't know whether the wolves would try to venture in here, but I don't see why they wouldn't. Two, we need to get those pickaxes Flor saw upstairs and break the gargoyles apart. Whatever the rock salt is doing may not last, and I don't think any of us want a rematch." I glanced at Flor, who was watching me intently. "And three—"

A stuffy voice echoed from upstairs. "Where in the *hell* has everyone gone?"

"Three," I repeated, "we need to keep an eye on Bertrand."

11

James volunteered to pickaxe the gargoyles while Flor and I dealt with the front door. Bertrand, who remained convinced the texts were somewhere in the monastery, went limping off with a make-shift torch in search of them. I let him, figuring it would keep him out of the way for the time being. It was the nighttime, when the rest of us would be sleeping, that he concerned me the most.

I grunted to the top of the stones Flor and I had piled against the timber we'd stood over the entrance. Ribs protesting where the gargoyle had driven its knee, I hefted a chunk of fallen pillar into the final space.

I exhaled. "There."

Flor blew a strand of hair from her eyes and assessed the pile, fists on her hips. "Now we use the rest of the timber to brace it."

I nodded wearily and climbed back down. Together, we stood a scavenged beam on end, wedged it against a fallen pillar set back from the entrance, and then lowered the other end against the piled-up stones at an angle. Opposite me,

Flor seemed to be handling the work with relative ease. I caught myself admiring the slender muscles along her arms.

"So..." I said as we lifted another beam, "now that there are no texts ... want to tell me what you're doing here?"

"You do not give up, do you?"

Her voice seemed to carry a flirtatious note of challenge. I peeked past the wooden beam to find the black eyes beneath her thick brows fixed on mine. A small smile teased her lips.

"On some questions, no," I said.

"What difference does it make why I am here? Like you say, there are no texts."

"Maybe I just want to trust you."

Far away, a wolf's howl went up. Flor looked from the sound to me, eyebrow cocked. "I saved you from them, didn't I?"

I opened my mouth, then closed it. She had a point.

With a cool dusky wind circling the courtyard, we set the final beam in place. Flor dusted off her hands and came forward until our legs were almost touching. "What is it you really want, Everson?"

I didn't realize I had been bracing my ribs on the right side until her hand slid under my sweat-damp shirt and over the ache. For someone who behaved with such dispassion in the face of danger, her palm blazed with heat. My body stiffened, then molded against her touch.

"I work for collectors," she said with a sigh. "A group with an interest in ancient texts and artifacts."

"Like a museum?" I asked, struggling to hold her face in focus. God, she felt good.

"No, they are private collectors." Her palm shifted to another sore spot. "They read the same article as you, James, and Bertrand. They hired me to see if the texts were here and to keep anyone from taking them."

I fought for a little analytical distance. Her secrecy, her military-grade rifle, her composure—and, yes, her terminal good looks. They all seemed consistent with someone who contracted out her services to the highest bidders. Which explained why she had been so concerned about Bertrand arriving here first.

"Were *you* supposed to take the texts?" I asked pointedly.

"I was only to keep them safe until the group could negotiate with the Romanian government for their purchase."

"Purchase?" Given their rarity, the texts would have cost a fortune. "Who is this group?"

"I am paid to do a job, not ask questions." She pressed closer. "Are you happy now?"

"Almost." I leaned toward her lips, a man anticipating his first taste of water after a six-month drought. I half expected a recoil and a sharp slap, but Flor's eyelids softened. Her chin tilted upward.

"I daresay, the wolves will have a devil of a time getting through that."

Flor and I jerked apart. A moment later, James appeared along the walkway, a pickaxe slung over one shoulder. *Awesome timing, mate.* He arrived beside us and looked the barricade up and down, nodding his approval. But when he turned to face us, his eyes were absent their usual joviality.

"Everything all right?" I asked.

He seemed to will his mouth into a smile. "Couldn't be better, mate." He clapped my shoulder with a little too much enthusiasm. "Hard work breaking up those gargoyles, but it's done."

Great. He had seen our near kiss, and now he was jealous. As if there wasn't already enough tension among the four of us.

"Where is Bertrand?" Flor asked.

We all peered around. A moment later, the Frenchman appeared at the far end of the courtyard. He had done away with his crutches and was limp-hopping toward us, a sweaty sweep of hair dangling over his eyes.

"Where are they?" he demanded. "Where are the texts?"

"We told you," James said. "The library and vault were empty when we arrived."

"That is a *lie!*" He stopped in front of us, the muscles around his eyes trembling with anger. "You took them!" He pointed at Flor but swept his arm back and forth to implicate all of us.

I stepped forward. "You need to calm down, bud. No one took anything."

"But they are here," he said. "I can *feel* them."

Flor waved a dismissive hand. "You are crazy."

His eyes jerked around until they locked on our packs, which we'd set beside a pillar. He hopped over and began tugging at the zippers of Flor's pack. "We will see who is crazy."

James seized the scruff of his jacket. "It's not polite to root through other people's belongings, mate."

Bertrand flailed his arms around, catching James in the mouth. James recoiled, the back of a hand to his lower lip, then held out both fists in a classic boxer's stance. Before I could intervene, Flor was behind Bertrand, a black pistol jammed against the back of his head.

"Let go of my pack."

I rushed up, palms showing. "Hey, hey, hey. Let's all just take a few deep breaths here. Bertrand, put her pack down." From his stooped-over position, Bertrand grunted and released the pack. "Okay. Now Flor. Let's put the gun away, hm?" Her lip curled, but she stepped away, clicking on the safety and holstering the pistol in the back of her pants.

I lowered my hands carefully, as though any sudden movement could shatter the fragile peace.

"I am not sharing my food with him," Flor declared.

"Neither am I." James glared down at Bertrand. "The mad bastard bloodied my lip."

"I do not want the food of *rogues*," Bertrand spat back. "It will probably be poisoned."

"Guys, look," I said. "Like it or not, we're stuck with one another until we make it back to the village. We're going to have to figure out a way to get along. I mean, it would be a shame to have survived the wolves and gargoyles only to end up killing each other." I chuckled at my own joke, but no one else joined in.

"But I *know* you have the texts," Bertrand said to us through clenched teeth.

"Here," Flor snapped. She unzipped her pack and, its mouth open for all to see, shoveled her hand around the contents: wads of clothes, a gas stove, metallic packets of food. "There, do you see? No texts, you crazy man."

Bertrand's lips pressed together.

To further dispel the tension, I opened my pack, too. While doing my own digging, my fingers encountered something cold and metallic. I withdrew a cone-shaped bullet, one that must have punctured my pack when Flor was shooting downstairs. I held it up in front of my face. Was that silver?

Flor's hand closed around it. "I am sorry about that."

"What about *his* pack?" Bertrand asked, cutting his eyes to James.

"Sorry, mate, but you don't get anything from me by throwing tantrums."

Flor sighed at the absurdity of what Bertrand was asking. "Do you think I would have let James take anything? Besides, I already checked."

James stared at her. "You did what?"

Bertrand pulled at his chin, no doubt recalling the sensation of a pistol against the back of his head. At last, he gave a single nod. "Fine." He straightened and tugged his jacket down. "But that does not change the fact that the texts are here. We will continue our search in the morning."

With that, he limped off to a prayer cell he'd apparently claimed for his quarters.

"Did he say 'we'?" James asked, glancing at the blood on the back of his hand. His bottom lip was beginning to pouch out where Bertrand had struck him. "Since when are we a team?"

I snorted. "Since he realized we're his best chance of finding whatever he's looking for."

Flor hoisted her pack onto a shoulder and hefted her titanium case. "If he wants to stay, it is his funeral. I am leaving in the morning."

"Right, well you can count me in," James said.

I felt their gazes cut to me. But my own eyes were on the flickering light in the doorway Bertrand had disappeared through. *They are here. I can feel them.* The Frenchman had looked fit for a Parisian asylum, and yet ... I felt something, too. The feeling was hard to explain—an insistent tapping at the base of my skull, an electric tingling over the hairs of my body—but what I sought was here, resonating with some essential part of me, beckoning.

"Everson?" Flor said.

I blinked from Bertrand's flickering doorway to the cold reason in Flor's eyes. I hesitated slightly before nodding.

"Yeah. I'll go in the morning too."

12

I zipped my jacket to my throat as I scuffed a slow patrol around the courtyard. James, Flor, and I had split the night into three shifts—as much to keep tabs on Bertrand as the monastery—and I had the midnight to three a.m. Except for the whistle of cold wind, Dolhasca was silent. No wolves at the door, no gargoyles in the library.

As I walked, my thoughts drifted like the membranes of mist wrapping the stone pillars.

I wondered about the pull of the monastery, about my conviction that the texts were here somewhere. And that energy in the vault? The last time I had felt anything like it had been in Grandpa's study.

Grandpa had never talked about that night again. In fact, scarcely a week after he sliced—and then apparently healed—my finger, the old East Manhattan townhouse he had owned for decades went on the market. A month later, we moved into a house in a boring suburb on Long Island.

Nana explained that Grandpa wanted to slow down, to cut back on his work. "We're both getting a little too old for the bustling city," she said. "And the schools are better out here."

Grandpa did seem to be home more. And I noticed early on that he left the door to his new study unlocked, often open. But it was a plain study, without a mysterious trunk or even bookcases. Just a desk with a typewriter, surrounded by a few metal filing cabinets. I never heard chanting or chilling voices from that study. Never experienced any strange energies. Gone, too, was much of the fascination and fear I used to feel in the man's presence.

Maybe I was just growing up.

THE SUMMER BEFORE I LEFT FOR COLLEGE, I CAME HOME FROM a date around midnight. I snapped on the living room light, surprised to find Grandpa in the easy chair beside the front window, wearing one of his dark linen suits, long legs crossed. He had never waited up for me before, but I didn't get that was what he was doing. He blinked sedately in the sudden light.

"Oh, hey," I said.

He nodded and said quietly, "Everson."

He brought his far hand from the side of the chair to his lap, and I saw he was palming a snifter of cognac. He swirled it gently, then took a sip. I had never known him to drink.

"Well, I'm gonna head up to bed," I said.

I had just reached the staircase when he spoke through his thick accent. "You are intent on returning to the city."

I twisted to face him. "Huh?" He so rarely remarked on my life, it took a moment to process his words. "Oh, yeah. Midtown College is one of the few with advanced programs in mythology studies. And I'll be on scholarship, which will offset the cost of—"

"You like the myths," he interrupted.

"Well, myths, iconography, symbols, ritual practices. Yeah."

"Why is that?"

Grandpa had always seemed distant. But it was the distance of one whose mind was other places. Maybe it was the tilt of his head now, but he looked different, as though he were more fully inside himself. I released the banister and took a step toward him.

"Because mythology speaks to something deeper," I said. "Something not quite seen. Like a huge ocean beneath a thin mantle." I watched Grandpa regarding me, a tuning fork-like resonance seeming to ring between our eyes. And was that a small smile on his lips? "Sometimes I feel that if I could, I don't know, learn the language of myth, I could access that place."

Grandpa's chuckle sounded hollow and knowing. He set the snifter on an end table, beside an old framed photo of his daughter, my mother, and beckoned with a pair of fingers. "Come here, Everson."

As I drew nearer, he held up both hands, palms showing, then moved one hand over the back of the other in an elegant gesture. When he showed me his palms again, a necklace and round pendant were in his right one.

I laughed. "How did you do that?"

He brought a slender finger to his lips. "You will wake Nana." But he was chuckling softly. "It is a simple sleight of hand."

He released the necklace, allowing it to slide into the sleeve of his suit, then repeated the trick, slowly. I peeked at his eyes, which seemed to glow with some memory. When his right hand circled the back of his left, his elbow flicked up so his sleeve deposited the necklace back into his palm. But the motion was so smooth, the timing so exact, I almost missed it.

He held the necklace out. "Here. It is for you."

I was surprised at its weight in my hand, the pendant a large coin.

"Iron," Grandpa said.

I studied the coin's symmetrical pattern. A circle with two squares inside, one rotated like a diamond. Intersecting lines, smaller marks on the corners. It looked like some sort of alchemy symbol. And whether or not it was my imagination, a force seemed to pulse from the cold metal.

"The necklace is an heirloom," Grandpa said. "It is meant to protect."

"Thank you." I glanced at his serious face. "But protect against what?"

Grandpa took the necklace by the chain and placed it around my neck, the coin settling over my sternum. As the subtle pulse from the metal radiated through bone—I wasn't imagining it now—the force became something deep and tidal, making me feel larger.

Grandpa looked me over and nodded, as though approving the fit of a suit.

"Wear it in the city, under your shirt." He wasn't asking. "And be very careful the words you speak."

I RETURNED FROM THE MEMORY, ONE HAND TOUCHING THE place on my chest where the coin hung. My headlamp illuminated a curving wall with deep stone shelves. The atmosphere tingled with energy. I blinked twice. *The hell?* I had been walking as I reminisced, yes, and I vaguely remembered having made my way down some steps. But ... I rotated slowly, my chest tightening at the idea.

I had come all the way to the vault of forbidden texts?

My heart leapt in panic. The curse of Dolhasca had led me here. I was sure of it. I was wheeling to rush back up the steps, to fresh air and space and safety, when I recognized the energy of the room. The night I had broken into Grandpa's old study, I had felt it near the bookcases. The same bookcases whose titles had changed when Grandpa spoke that word.

Svelare.

The thought of it seemed to send a small shudder around the room, and I could have sworn something fluttered on the verge of my vision, deep in the bookshelves. Gone now, but it had looked as though something was trying to take form.

I drew in my breath, hesitated on Grandpa's warning—

Be very careful the words you speak.

—and released the word.

"*Svelare.*"

The syllables vibrated from my mouth, establishing a kind of tonal resonance in the vault. Deep in the shelves, oscillations. I blinked twice and shone my headlamp around. A second ago, the shelves had been empty. Now they were crowded with leather-bound books.

Shut the fuck up.

I reached forward and pulled one from its slot. The dark leather cover was extraordinarily well preserved. I opened it to the first hand-written page—calligraphy in old Latin. Translated, it read, *Gospel of the Egyptians*, an early Christian text believed lost.

"I don't believe this," I whispered.

Behind me, something scuffed over stone. I wheeled, a

shout lodged in my throat. Expecting gargoyles, I was surprised to find a flash of lenses. But the lenses weren't aimed at me. They stared around the vault.

"They are here," Bertrand marveled, removing his glasses as he emerged from the staircase. "By God, they are here."

13

Bertrand shoved past me and pulled down a book, his lighter flickering over the pages. "Oh my, a Sappho," he said. "Composed hundreds of years before Christ." He seemed to be speaking more to himself than to me. "And this..." He pulled and opened a second book. "Ha-haa! Yes, this is an old Persian prayer book, translated into a liturgical Latin—the only one of its kind."

I looked from him to the books, stunned by the sudden appearance of both. Bertrand must have slipped from his room and followed me. I returned the book I had pulled and scanned the others. *The Book of Souls* would be among them, and something told me I needed to find it before Bertrand did.

"It is a treasure," he said of the collection. "A treasure!"

I was reaching for another book when he seized my wrist. He pulled himself close until I could smell his sour sweat. In a thick whispered voice, he said, "We must not tell the others."

"You want to keep this from them?" I asked. "Besides being impossible, we agreed to share our findings."

"*You* agreed to share. Not me."

I yanked my arm from his grasp. "I don't give a damn what you did or didn't agree to. We'd both be decomposing right now if Flor and James hadn't saved us from the wolves and gargoyles."

He looked from me to the books, shadows climbing over his bony face. "Fine. We tell them. But not tonight. Not until we catalogue the collection."

Before I could answer, he shed his pack and began digging through it. When he straightened he was holding two notepads and a pair of pens. He pushed one of each into my hands. "You begin on that side. I will start over here. Then we check each other's work. Ensure there are no omissions."

Whether or not the man was a phony, Bertrand had proven his proficiency in old Greek and Latin as well as in ancient texts. And his proposal held merit. By working through the night, we could complete a catalogue by the morning, one the four of us could work from for the next several days. Plus, it would prevent anyone—including Bertrand—from making off with a text.

I nodded, my phobia returning to sit on my chest. "All right."

My list grew faster than Bertrand's, mostly because he was stopping to peruse the texts, while I was on a mission to find a single book. I hid this by working through the collection systematically. Two hours before dawn, eyes dry and strained, fingertips chaffed, I pulled down a thick tome. Even before peering on the black leather cover, its weight spoke to me. A symbol, similar to that on my coin pendant, had been burned into the leather.

On the first page, large letters confirmed my growing certainty: *Liber de Animis.* Book of Souls.

Like a child, I sat cross-legged with the book. The rest of

the vault seemed to draw back, as though on tracks. Breathless, I read the first line: *"Herein lie the Grimoires sacred to the Line of Michael, Defender of Souls."*

I raised my gaze to Bertrand, who was absorbed in his own book. Holding him there, I slid the *Book of Souls* into a sleeve in the back of my pack where the internal frame had been. I covered the opening with a sweatshirt, then stood and pulled another book from the shelf.

When Bertrand and I switched pads an hour later, he looked over my list and smiled companionably. "Oh, the knowledge that will come from these works, Everson. It will alter the trajectory of scholarship. Open new avenues of thought." He squinted up the steps. "I am glad it was you who found them and not the others."

"Oh, yeah?"

"You are green, but at least you are an academic."

"Well, James too," I pointed out. "At Oxford."

Bertrand sniffed. "So he claims."

"What do you mean?"

"I asked him about a professor in his department. He talked like he knew him, but I could tell by his face he did not."

I thought about that. Flor had said his story checked out. Then again, she had also said Bertrand was a fraud—and yet here he was, displaying an interest and understanding of the texts that went far beyond a layman's. As though picking up on my thoughts, Bertrand sniffed again.

"I do not trust the Spaniard, either. I believe she means to steal these. We must watch them closely, Everson. Even a single missing text will compromise what might be gained here. The works must be studied as a whole."

I nodded, then lifted my pack with the hidden book and turned it so the sleeve was against the wall.

"But where did they come from?" James asked, looking from the texts to Bertrand and me. "They weren't here yesterday. How's this possible?"

"How are gargoyles coming to life possible?" I replied, bristling at the suspicion in James's voice. "Hell if I know. One minute the shelves were empty, and then they were full. In any case, Bertrand and I catalogued the collection and made lists." I handed one each to James and Flor.

"Why didn't you wake us?" Flor asked, her eyes moving down the entries.

I searched for an answer that wouldn't sound defensive or patronizing. But before I could speak, Bertrand spat, "Because in the confusion you would have stolen what you wanted."

"How do we know you didn't do the same?" Flor shot back.

"Guys, c'mon," I said. "We checked each other's work." Standing so that my legs blocked my pack, I clapped my hands, anxious to change the subject. "All right, there are a lot of books but not a lot of time. So here are the ground rules. Find the ones you're interested in. They can be checked out two at a time and taken anywhere in the monastery. But they must be returned by the next morning to give someone else a chance to read them. Are we all agreed?"

Seeing nothing objectionable in that, James and Flor nodded.

I chose two books, one because it contained a legend that went into the origins of a Saint Michael, possibly the one referenced in the *Book of Souls*. The second was the approximate size and weight of the stolen tome in my bag.

I left my traveling companions to their selections,

climbing back up to the prayer cell where I had slept the first part of last night. There, I sat in a shadowy corner, facing the door. After listening to ensure no one was coming, I pulled the *Book of Souls* from my backpack and shoved the other one into its place.

Energy hummed over the book's binding, like a life force. The same force that had pulled me back to the vault last night.

I opened the cover and began to read.

14

The sound of crying pulled me from my reading. I looked up from the book, half startled to find a room around me, so completely had I fallen into the book's mind-bending world of prisms and power lines, spells and symbols, summonings and supernatural beings—Grandpa's world. Mystifying and yet oddly familiar.

Was this what Grandpa had been getting at ten years ago when he spoke of *those of our blood*?

The only clues to Grandpa's mysterious existence were the things I had observed from his closet when I was thirteen and the few odd items I found rummaging around the house after his death. A death that lacked the mystery of his life. He was struck by a car while crossing a street near our house, a no-fault case of him stepping from between two parked SUVs at the very moment a bee flew into the face of an oncoming driver. The distressed woman, on her way to pick up her son from nursery school, had the welt and stinger to prove it.

Just one of those things.

Among the items I found was Grandpa's cane, his ring with the dragon, and rolled up beside some maps in the back of his closet, an old poster advertising "Asmus the Great! Master Magician!"

The poster depicted a tuxedo-clad man with rosy cheeks reaching into a top hat. He looked like a younger version of Grandpa. Remembering the sleight-of-hand trick Grandpa had taught me, I wondered if he'd done a stint with "Barnum's American Museum," the advertised venue. There *had* been a Barnum's Museum in the city, I would later learn—the only problem was that it had burned to the ground in 1868. Had Grandpa's *grandpa* been the stage magician?

There was no one around to ask. A month after Grandpa's death, Nana succumbed to pneumonia, though I always suspected heartbreak to have played its part.

The muffled crying started up again. I hid the book in my pack, swapping it for the one I'd check out, and consulted my watch. More than ten hours had passed since I'd begun reading.

Outside my room, the gray light of dusk fell onto the courtyard. I had been dimly aware of the others coming and going throughout the day, no doubt relaying texts to and from the vault. Across the open space, the light of a small fire danced from Bertrand's room, and I could hear his muttering voice. But the crying was coming from the room beside mine.

I craned my neck through the doorway, surprised to find Flor facedown on her bedding in the corner of the dormitory, hair splayed over the forearm she was sobbing against.

"Hey," I said softly. "Everything all right?"

She sniffled and wiped her eyes with her sleeping bag. Papers were strewn around her as though thrown in frustration.

"No," she said. "Everything is awful."

Though Bertrand's warning about her lingered in my mind, she sounded more fragile than I had ever heard her. I hadn't even thought fragility a part of her makeup. I lowered myself to the edge of her sleeping pad. "Well, if you tell me what's going on, maybe I can help."

With a long sniff, Flor sat up and tucked her hair behind her ears. She glanced up at me with damp, red-rimmed eyes —she hadn't been acting—then began gathering the strewn papers.

"This is the list I was given by the collectors," she said. "The texts I was to make sure were here. But except for a few, the names on their list do not match the names on the one you gave me."

"May I?" I asked. When she handed me the lists, I looked them over. "Ah, the names the collectors gave you are in orthodox Latin. Understandable. But the titles of the texts are in a Latin used by the monks, some of the words entirely different. So, let's see..." I pulled a pen from my shirt pocket as I consulted both lists. "This matches this here." I wrote a small letter *a* beside both titles. "And this one matches this." Beside those, I penned a *b*.

Flor watched me work, her body gradually conforming to the side of mine. Not an unpleasant feeling. I continued until I had accounted for all of the titles on the list she had brought with her. All save one.

"You see?" I smiled over at her. "Nothing to be upset about."

"What about this one?" she asked, indicating the *Book of Souls*.

"It's not here, apparently."

Her glistening gaze searched my eyes before falling to my lips. In the next moment, her mouth was pressed against mine, fingers sliding into my hair. I leaned into the kiss, dizzy with her aggression, her strong, sensual taste. She broke back suddenly, hands holding the sides of my head.

"I have wanted this since I met you."

I nodded dazedly, falling into her lips again. She pulled me on top of her, fingers unclasping the buttons of my shirt. I held her cheeks, her neck, squeezed the muscles of her upper back.

"You were right, love," a voice said.

I sat up and twisted around to find James standing inside the doorway, a hard gleam in his eyes. As I buttoned my shirt back, I heard Flor scoot off the bedding behind me. With the shock of intrusion, I hadn't paid attention to James's actual words. "Ever heard of knocking," I muttered.

"Is that it?" Flor asked.

When James stepped into the light, I saw he was holding the *Book of Souls*.

"I imagine so," he said. "Everson had it stuffed in his pack. He can verify it, though."

I looked from James to Flor, who was standing now—and pointing her pistol at me. "Is that the missing book?" she asked. Her hair was mussed from our two minutes of heaven, but her voice was ice cold.

I stammered silently for a second, my lips still throbbing. "What in the hell is going on?"

"I'm sorry, Everson," she said. "We were hired to do a job."

"*We?*" My eyes flicked between them, head spinning with the unreality of what was happening. "You're working together?"

James gave a hard smile as he paced around me to Flor. Pulling her to his side, he kissed her crown with the familiarity of a lover. "As I said, two heads are better than one."

"Is it the missing book?" Flor repeated.

"Get him to tell you," I said bitterly. "James speaks old Lat..." I stopped, remembering how he had found the inscription outside the vault of forbidden texts but not actually translated it. "You don't, do you? You just know that one line you fed me at the pension."

The manuscripts are said to be in archaic Latin.

"Past tense," James corrected me. "I've already forgotten it."

I sighed. Who knew how long they'd been hanging out in the village, waiting for an unwitting researcher to show up and act as their translator, to ensure they would locate the correct texts. They had no doubt tried Bertrand, who rightly saw them as trouble—hence their need to impugn his character. Everson Croft on the other hand? Classic dupe. I fell for the whole damned thing, from Flor's pretended reluctance to travel together, to her supposed Google search, to her hot damsel in distress act. My gaze moved across the papers I had notated for her.

"I believe Flor asked you a question," James said. "Is this the missing book?"

I looked from the bore of Flor's pistol to the tome in James's hand. I remembered what I had felt while reading it, the shifting deep inside me, like wooden boxes being pushed from a trapdoor, one that opened onto the same subterranean ocean I had described to Grandpa. The book didn't belong to them, and I sensed the powerful book felt the same way.

"What will you do with it?" I asked.

James chuckled. "I'll take that as a *yes*." He flipped open the book and thumbed through the pages irreverently. "We'll be taking it, of course. Taking them all. We have very wealthy collectors in the wings. Flor wasn't lying about that. Just about them wanting to purchase the collection from the Romanian government."

"Would you consider leaving that one?"

"Heavens, no." James clapped the book closed and tucked

it under an arm. "It's the one the collectors are most interested in."

Heat burned in my cheeks. "So what now?"

"We have to send you and Bertrand out, I'm afraid," James said.

"Feed us to the wolves," I said numbly.

"Messy for you, but rather tidy for us."

Flor huffed. "You two are talking too much. The alternative is I shoot you."

"How sweet," I muttered.

James set the *Book of Souls* down and lifted Flor's rifle. It was no accident she was carrying silver ammo, or that James had packed rock-salt necklaces. This was their work—looting ancient sites, some of them cursed, no doubt. "Let's go," James said. "We'll pick up Bertrand on the way."

"Can I grab my backpack, at least?"

"No." Flor jabbed me in the side with the pistol, sending a spear through one of the spots she'd soothed last night. "Move your ass."

I considered running as I stumbled into the courtyard, but there was nowhere *to* run. Doing so would just get me shot. Bertrand's and my best chance would be to do as they said. Once outside, we could scale a tree and wait until morning, attempt the journey down to the village then. It seemed a reasonable plan until I remembered the bear-like paws on the wolves. Something told me they would use them to climb after us.

We arrived at Bertrand's room and found him sitting in a corner, scribbling in a notepad on his propped-up knees. His hair jerked as he consulted open texts on either side of him.

"Check out time," James called.

Bertrand's face shot up, his eyes seeming to refocus from some distant realm. He swept his hair to one side and squinted at the pointed weapons, which glinted in the light of his small fire. "What is the meaning of this?"

"You were right," I told him. "They're a couple of scoundrels. They're going to send us out to the wolves and take the books to some collector so they can buy themselves iPods and fancy shoes."

"Oh, don't be such a poor sport," James said. "If you'd shown yourself a little more agreeable to our line of work, why, we might have asked you to join us. We're in need of a new translator."

I remembered my reaction at dinner in the village when Flor suggested we split the spoils. Another test.

"Why?" I growled. "What happened to your last one?"

"We had a disagreement," Flor said. "Now get moving. Both of you."

I had expected Bertrand to put up a fight, but he was on his hands and knees gathering his notepads.

"Leave them," Flor ordered. "They will do you no good out there."

"Oh, let him have them, love," James whispered. "It'll occupy his hands and we can get them out of here with less fuss."

Bertrand hobbled up beside me, notepads pressed to his chest, eyes shifting wildly. The discovery of the texts had meant everything to him. "They will not get away with this," he spat. "I will be *damned* if they get away with this."

"Keep cool," I whispered. "We'll figure out something once we're outside."

He ignored me, rifling through his notepads as James and Flor prodded us into the courtyard. The barricaded entrance wasn't entirely barricaded anymore, I saw. Stones had been moved and one of the timber beams set aside for Bertrand and me to squeeze through. The cold wind funneling into the monastery carried the cries of wolves. Not close, but not too distant, either.

Beside me, Bertrand's grumbling turned to hard mutters.

"Stay cool," I repeated distractedly, trying to remember the terrain outside the monastery. If we could find a cave in the rock face, a place to fortify ourselves, we had a slim chance of surviving the night.

Bertrand's muttering rose in pitch.

"Shut up," Flor said—which were my thoughts, as well. He was going to get us both ventilated. But when I turned, I found that he was no longer muttering for muttering's sake. He was reading from one of his notepads. And I recognized the words. The chant was an incantation meant to summon something dark and powerful, an idea that might have seemed insane to me only a few days ago.

"Be careful," I whispered, remembering a warning inside the *Book of Souls*. "Whatever you call up you're going to have to put back down."

But the atmosphere of the monastery was already changing. Something was sucking out the oxygen, making it hard to breathe. And an unpleasant smell was rising. A sickly sweet odor that stuck like barbs in my throat. The odor of whatever Bertrand was summoning, I realized.

"The Frenchman first," Flor said as we arrived at the entranceway. "I cannot stand the sight of him any longer."

Bertrand snapped straight, the notepads spilling from his arms. He remained like that, eyes large and staring, until I thought he was having a seizure. I grabbed his rigid left arm and gave it a shake.

"Bertrand?"

When he turned, I released him and staggered back a step. Blackness had spread over his eyes like spilled ink. And his lips were stretching from his teeth, forming a smile so large it looked agonizing.

"You can no longer stand the sight of Bertrand?" he said to Flor in an alien voice, as though something was humming deep in his throat. "Well perhaps he can no longer stand the sight of *you*."

His smile unhinged and a droning black cloud shot from his mouth. Wasps, I realized in horror. Flor had time to scream before the wasps swarmed her face and smothered her cries.

15

"S-stop that." James's huge eyes looked from Flor's collapsed body to Bertrand—or whatever Bertrand had become. Seeming to remember he was holding a rifle, James raised it. "Stop! Get them off her!"

Bertrand laughed. "As you wish."

He waved a hand and the hundreds upon hundreds of wasps lifted from Flor and swarmed James. He screamed and stumbled backwards, rifle shots cracking as though the swarm was a being whose heart he might pierce. I crouched beside Flor and moved the limp arm from across her face. She looked nothing like the woman of only moments ago. Her face had become a disfiguration of red welts, eyes a pair of glistening lines, lips a fruit that had burst in the sun.

Oh God. I lowered her lifeless arm.

Above me, Bertrand laughed, the sound a sick buzzing. "You dare insult a Wasp Demon, mother of the brood, matron of death." I pressed a forearm to my nose, the cloying smell threatening to choke me.

"Help me, Everson!" James shrieked above the thickening swarm. "For God's sake, *help me!*"

He tripped over a section of pillar. As he fell onto his back, the wasps descended over his blondness like a black blanket, muffling his cries. A moment later, his spastic arms collapsed out to his sides, the spent rifle clacking against stone.

With Bertrand's back to me, I left Flor's body and edged toward the monastery entrance. The wasps rose from James and returned to Bertrand, funneling into his mouth. There had clearly been another spell book in the collection, a dark one that Bertrand had gotten his hands on. I didn't know how possessions worked exactly, didn't know how much of Bertrand remained in his body. But I wasn't planning on sticking around to find out.

I was almost to the opening when eyes flashed from the darkness beyond, and a thick, snapping snout lunged into the space.

"Damn!" I cried, stumbling backwards.

Front legs squeezed through as the wolf wriggled and pushed his head in. More fanged snouts jabbed into the surrounding gaps. I shot a glance back at Bertrand. He was finger-combing his hair with both hands, as though cleaning a pair of antennas. My gaze flew around the courtyard. All the monastery's rooms were doorless. No places to shut out the wolves—or Bertrand. And my pepper spray would only keep them at bay for so long.

The Book of Souls, I thought.

I launched into a run toward the room where James had left it.

Behind me, the wolf burst inside with a jagged cry, his thick nails scratching over the stone, gaining speed. But a fresh buzzing was climbing over the sounds of the wolves.

"Fly, my beauties," Bertrand said. "Kill them."

Yes, please do.

"The human, too."

Crap.

I seized the side of the dormitory doorway with one hand and swung myself into Flor's old room. The wolf overshot the door, skittering as he tried to brake. I kicked past Flor's bag and titanium case, scooped up the *Book of Souls,* and pressed my back to the wall. I opened the book and flipped to the rear. Most of the book's spells required something called a casting prism and Words of Power.

But not summonings.

A wasp landed on my neck, sending a molten barb down to my spine. I crushed it with my shoulder and turned more pages. Out in the courtyard, sharp cries and yelps went up in the thickening swarm. But the swarm hadn't reached me—or the wolf who had been on my heels. A low growl sounded from the doorway. I glanced up to find the beast stalking toward me, ears twitching in the haze of wasps, impervious to their stings. Something told me this was the Alpha. Raising a leg in preparation to kick, I dropped my gaze to the page before me.

"*Thelonious,*" I boomed, pushing energy into the word, making each syllable count. I didn't know who or what I was invoking, but when the alternative was certain death, there was no time to be choosy. "*I beseech you for aid,*" I said in the old Latin. "*I offer myself as a vessel in exchange.*"

Creamy white light fluttered on the verge of my vision, then roared in, like a strong surf. I could no longer see the wolf, the wasps, the room, the book in my own hands. Just the frothy light that rolled up in layers, growing thicker. From beneath the roaring light came a slow, throbbing sound, like a bass line. The sound was compelling, arousing. I could have been inside a West Village jazz club, men and women grooving and bumping bodies.

"Yesss?" came a rich voice.

I squinted at where the creamy light seemed to thicken around a large, inchoate form. A Buddha. It was clear, though, that this Buddha was no esthetic. Sensual forms moved around his corpulent body, attending to his needs, which seemed to include food, drink ... other things.

"Are you Thelonious?" I asked.

"Indeed," he replied with a pleasant bass laugh. He seemed benign, at least.

"I need your help."

Though my heart beat slammed through my words, I sensed Thelonious had drawn me into some sort of parallel plane, outside space and time.

"I'd say so." Feminine titters accompanied the spirit's rumbling laughter. "But I'm busy at the moment."

"Look, I'm only twenty-three," I babbled. "My life's not perfect, but I'm not ready for it to end. I live in New York—the greatest city on Earth. I love my chosen field. I'm the youngest PhD candidate in my department and just a thesis away from graduating. I'm a, ah, a lifelong Mets fan—and they're actually doing well this year." I was really grasping now, but if he rejected my appeal and cast me back, I was a dead man. Simple as that.

Thelonious chuckled. "Long time since I've been in New York. Are there still dance halls?"

"Oh man, a ton."

"And the women?"

"Millions, and they're all beautiful."

He made a noise of interest, then heaved himself up, sending his harem streaming away. "And you say you're a young man?" He circled me as though in assessment.

"Learned ... enjoys sport." He stopped in front of me. "If I help you this once, you'll give yourself as a vessel for all time?"

I hesitated. "And what does that entail, exactly?"

He rumbled more laughter as something like a hand descended onto my shoulder. "Nothing but good times."

"So we'll be running my body like, what, a time share?"

"When the itch for city life needs scratching, Thelonious will come calling."

"Otherwise, my body's my own?"

"One hundred percent."

"And you won't be doing anything illegal in here, right?"

He released more rich laughter. "Not unless you consider loving and living crimes."

As the bass line and creamy lights of his world throbbed through me, I found myself nodding. Maybe an occasional visit by Thelonious would do me good, get me out of my studio apartment now and again. Given my sad social life, it certainly couldn't make things worse.

"All right," I said, not wanting to think about it too hard. "I agree to your terms. In exchange for helping me with the wolves and wasp demon, I pledge myself as your vessel, whenever the, um ... itch needs scratching." I probably should have asked for an estimate on how often that would be.

"Right on, brother. Right on."

Thelonious gave me the equivalent of a soul shake, and I was back in the monastery, the *Book of Souls* open in my hands, one leg raised, and a huge wolf stalking me through a growing fog of wasps.

"Kill them all!" Bertrand cried from the courtyard, his voice a phlegmy buzz now, as though he were choking on the wasps he spawned. The ensuing laughter sounded like someone coughing up a lung.

I glanced around for my own summoned being, wincing as another wasp stung my brow.

"Thelonious?"

16

The *Book of Souls* tumbled from my trembling hands. Three more stings seared my upper back, spreading like a deep burn. I flailed to slap the wasps away, the motion exciting the wolf. He snarled and charged.

I cringed against the wall and kicked out. My heel caught the wolf's jaw, harder than I'd struck anything in my life. Bone crunched, and the two-hundred-pound wolf staggered backwards. He righted himself drunkenly, a rope of pink saliva hanging from his crooked mouth.

"That's right!" I cried, my fear swelling into anger. "There's more where that came from."

Nice one, a bass voice rumbled.

"Thelonious!"

Either my body was growing or my share of it becoming smaller as the chuckling spirit eased all the way in. The warm, creamy light from earlier undulated through me—an ecstatic force of strength and virulence. As its aura pulsed from me, the attacking wasps wavered and fell to the stone floor.

We stepped toward the wolf, wasp husks crunching

underfoot. The Alpha backed away like a scolded house dog, whimpering and trailing urine. When his haunches hit a wall, he pressed himself flat. I—or rather, Thelonious— laughed and reached down to scratch his ear, the hair surprisingly smooth. The Alpha licked our hand before succumbing to his stings.

"Incubus!" Out in the courtyard, Bertrand stood in a black storm of wasps, arms open, clothes crawling. "Leave the human to his fate."

"What are you prepared to deal for him?" Thelonious asked through my mouth.

Hey! I said. *You and I are already locked into a deal!*

Ignoring me, Thelonious walked us through the storm, his creamy light illuminating the courtyard in swimmy waves. Wasps peppered us from all sides only to drop in a steady hail. It was like being inside an armored tank, but one I had no control over and that might eject me at any moment.

"I will spare you the agony of feeling him die, incubus," Bertrand answered. "Now leave him to me!"

Thelonious shook his head. "Bad deal."

He thrust my arms forward, and I watched my hands close around Bertrand's throat. Wasps writhed beneath his skin where I squeezed. His enormous black eyes startled, but more in insult it seemed than pain. He opened his mouth, unleashing another torrent of insects. As I tried to wince back, Thelonious only seemed to grow larger and more powerful.

"Go back to your own joint." He forced the possessed Frenchman to his knees. Bertrand buzz-shrieked, his arms breaking into more wasps as he beat at our hands. "You're killing the mood here," Thelonious said.

In a final explosion of dying wasps, the rest of Bertrand came apart. But something grotesque remained—a huge queen wasp, curled at his core. Her sticky wings opened out and vibrated, the sudden wind pushing us back. With an angry scream, the queen rose, as though to escape the monastery through the open-air courtyard. But Thelonious jumped and seized her by a rear leg.

Watch the stinger!

I had hardly formed the thought when the stinger skewered my right forearm. I clenched my teeth, but the excruciating pain never came. "The sharper the thorn," Thelonious said, pulling out the stinger and snapping it from the queen's body. "The sweeter the fruit."

Um ... what?

Thelonious tossed the stinger away and dragged the queen to the courtyard floor, flipping her so her wings were pinned beneath her. The queen kicked her legs and rotated her alien head.

Wait, you're not planning on...

With a rumbling purr, Thelonious brought his mouth —*our* mouth—down to the queens pincher jaws.

Oh God, you are.

I tried to recoil, to twist my head away, but an instant before our lips closed around the gnashing mandibles, Thelonious stopped and began to draw from her. The queen strained back, but her essence was leaving her, being pulled into Thelonious. Hers was a spiny, spiteful essence, full of poison, but at its center was a single, sweet drop. The feminine nectar Thelonious was after.

When the queen fell still, Thelonious rolled us off her, contented. "That was all right," he rumbled.

Yeah, for you, maybe. I peeked over at the dead queen. *Is this going to be par for the course?*

"Know something, young blood?" he said in a languid voice. "Believe I'm gonna enjoy this partnership."

Thelonious's creamy white energy that had seemed so benign and good-time a moment before collapsed into something dense and black. I choked as it burrowed deeper into me, like a parasite, affixing itself to my soul with hundreds of piercing hooks. The shock of the binding pitched my mind into an oblivion as pitiless as the being I had just bargained with.

17

I cracked my eyes open onto a diffusion of pale light. I was peering at the sky above the courtyard, the sun a white smear beyond a wash of gray clouds. I pushed myself up, wincing from my wasp stings, and squinted around. The wasps and demon were gone—as though evaporated into mist—but not their victims. The bodies of a dozen or more large wolves lay stiff and bloated. Near the entrance, I spotted James and Flor, where they had fallen.

I staggered to my feet, recalling all that had happened last night. The deception, Bertrand's summoning, Thelonious. I could feel the incubus spirit now, a dark twining, a stain on my soul.

"You are a fool."

I wheeled to find a tall man stepping from Flor's room. Though he was without his peasant hat and no longer spoke in broken English, I recognized him by his battered rubber boots. The cart driver paced into the courtyard, The *Book of Souls* open in his hands.

"I told you the journey would be your death," he said.

I didn't like his threatening tone. "Who are you?" I asked, stooping for a rock.

He raised his disfigured face from the book. When I drew back the rock in warning, he flicked his fingers and uttered something. An invisible force hit my hand, knocking the rock away.

"You are the grandson of Asmus Croft." He appraised me with sober eyes, his left one cloudy from the wolf attack.

I rubbed my hand. "You knew him?"

"Of course." The dragon ring on his third finger gleamed dully as he closed the book. "He was a member of the Order, a principal in the war against the Inquisition, a grand mage."

"A wizard?"

The man's statement seemed to affirm something I had known on a cellular level, and it explained so much. There was no time to marvel, though. I sensed danger around the man. He had made the perilous journey through the forest, after all, and just disarmed me with a word and gesture.

"Who *are* you?" I glanced around. "What are you doing here?"

"I am called Lazlo. I am a Keeper of the Books."

"Keeper of...?" I quickly fit the pieces together. "So you're the one who hid the books in the vault? Wh-who set up the spell to animate the gargoyles?" I recalled the battered looters downstairs and stepped back.

"Books must be kept from certain hands." He tapped his scarred temple as he strode forward. "Certain minds."

"Look, I'll leave here and never come back, never talk about the texts again. I-I'll forget everything I saw. I promise."

When Lazlo arrived in front of me, I sensed a being who was much older than he appeared. And had he said something about a war against the Inquisition? Could that have been the "awful war" Nana mentioned? But the Inquisition was centuries ago. My mind seized on the poster in Grandpa's closet, the one advertising "Asmus the Great!" at Barnum's American Museum. The depicted stage magician hadn't been his grandfather. It had been Grandpa himself.

"You have read the Words," Lazlo said. "You have spoken them. And yet here you stand while your friends are fallen." His gaze shifted from James to Flor, then to the pile of clothes that had belonged to Bertrand. "It means you are a magic born, like your grandfather."

"What?"

"But you are still a fool. You made an accord with an ancient being, one that would have consumed a lesser soul. Such an accord might be tempered with practice, but it can never be unbound. You are marked for all time, Everson Croft." The judgment in his tone made me shudder. "I have contacted those more knowledgeable in such matters. I am waiting to hear from them."

"Hear what?"

"Whether to train you into our Order or to destroy you."

———

I ONCE WONDERED WHAT IT WAS LIKE FOR A MAN AWAITING execution to hear whether a last-minute stay had been granted. Now I knew. It was a hard stone in the pit of my stomach. A prickling nausea. A constant disbelieving. While Lazlo took care of the bodies, I spent the day confined to my prayer cell—organizing my pack, reflecting on my life, and, yes, praying.

Praying and wondering.

Grandpa must have suspected I was a magic born, as Lazlo put it. But why hadn't he said anything? Or had he? I remembered him placing the necklace with the heavy coin around my neck. *Wear it in the city, under your shirt. And be very careful the words you speak.*

A warning. But against what?

He had given me something else of his, the day before his death, though I hadn't recognized it at the time.

The day was Sunday. I had ridden the train in from the city for the weekend. Nana and I attended morning Mass at the neighborhood cathedral, one that never seemed to resonate for me in the same way St. Martin's in Manhattan had. Afterwards, when Nana had gone upstairs for her nap, Grandpa called me into his study.

"Everson," he said, turning toward me from his desk. His cane rested across his long knees, the same cane he had carried since as far back as I could remember, whose hidden blade had once bitten my finger. "It seems I am having trouble opening it. Would you try?"

A bracing fear seized me, similar to the one I had felt upon being discovered in his closet. I hadn't seen the blade since that night, almost eight years before, and I wasn't sure I wanted to see it again.

"Yeah ... sure."

"Hold it at the top and middle, like this."

I did as Grandpa said, the wood smooth and cool in my uncertain grip.

"Now do not think about it," he said. "Just pull."

The cane seemed to catch at first. No, clench. It was clenching. But after another moment, the wood warming in my hands, it released, sliding apart in a single smooth stroke. I looked at the handsome sword I held in my right hand and then at the staff in my left. I was surprised at how comforting their weight felt, like they were extensions of my arms.

But more than that, they felt ... empowering.

"Very good," Grandpa said, taking them back from me. He

slid the sword home again, the two parts he had wanted me to separate slotting along an invisible seam. "It remembers you."

Remembers?

A flash of him thumbing away my blood and running it along the sword blade came back to me. But before I could ask what he meant, Grandpa turned to his desk. "If you'll excuse me, Everson, I have some things to tie up now."

Our final conversation. So little said—and yet maybe that had been the point.

I was pulled from the memory by a shadow in the doorway. I turned to find Lazlo's tall form approaching, the pale scars across his face glowing in the late light. I stood at rigid attention.

"I have heard," he said, his voice grave.

I almost couldn't form the single syllable, my mouth was so dry. "And?"

He stepped all the way into the room. Cold power seemed to warp the air around his hands. My heart beat like a dusty drum, but I refused to cower. Whatever the answer, I sensed he had been right. The journey to Dolhasca had been my death. The old Everson Croft was no more.

"As decreed by the Order," Lazlo said, "I am to initiate you into training tonight."

THE END

But be sure to catch up with Everson Croft in his next novella, Siren Call, *or his first full-length novel,* Demon Moon. *Keep reading for a preview...*

DEMON MOON

A PREVIEW OF PROF CROFT BOOK 1

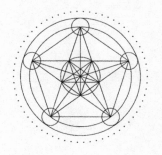

I blew out a curse as the first cold droplets of rain pelted my face and punched through my magic. As if I wasn't already running late.

Making an umbrella of my coat collar, I stooped into a run, skirting bags of garbage that swelled from the fronts of row houses like pustules, but it was no use. The downpour that blackened the sidewalk and drove rats from the festering piles also broke apart my hunting spell.

And it had been one of my better ones.

I took refuge on a crumbling porch and shook out my coat. I was in the pit of the East Village, and it stunk. Except for a flicker of street light, the block was midnight dark, the building across the way a brick shell, hollowed out by arson. Not the domicile of the conjurer I needed to stop. Or more likely save.

Assuming I could find him now.

"Seguire," I said in a low, thrumming voice.

Most hunting spells worked like a dowsing rod, pulling the user toward the source of something. In this case, taboo magic. But reliable hunting spells, such as those needed to navigate New York's convoluted streets, required time to prepare. And even then they were delicate.

"Seguire," I repeated, louder.

Though the storm was already sweeping off, the spell refused to take shape again. I swore under my breath. Magic and moving water made poor bedfellows. And here I'd dropped a fat hundred on the booster: ground narwhal tusk. Sunk cost, I thought bitterly as I hustled back to the sidewalk. There were a lot of those in wizardry, my svelte wallet the proof.

Splashing in the direction I'd been pulled before the cloudburst, I gave up on the hunting spell and resorted to twenty-twenty vision, scanning passing buildings for signs of life.

As the sidewalks thickened with larger mounds of garbage, the rats became more territorial. I knocked aside several with my walking cane. The soul eaters that hunkered like shadows in the below-ground stairwells weren't quite so bold. They watched with hollow eyes before shrinking from the protective power of my necklace, in search of weaker, drug-addled prey. Luckily for them, post-Crash New York was a boomtown for chemical addiction.

Unfortunately for me, the financial crash had also made a growth stock of amateur conjurers.

They tended to be men and women seeking lost money or means—or simply some meaning where their prior faith, whether spiritual or material, seemed to have failed them. Understandable, certainly, but as far as my work went, a royal pain in the ass. Most mortals could only access the nether realms, and shallowly at that. In their fat-fingered efforts, they called up grubby creatures better left undisturbed. Ones more inclined to make a sopping meal of a conjurer's heart than grant his material wishes.

Trust me, it wasn't pretty.

Neither was the job of casting the charming beings back to their realms, but it was the job I'd been decreed. I had some nice acid burns and a missing right ear lobe to prove it. A business card might have read:

Everson Croft
Wizard Garbage Collector

Nice, huh? But unlike the city's striking sanitation workers, I couldn't just walk off the job.

Small messes became big messes, and in magical terms, that was a recipe for ruin. The apocalyptic kind. Better to scoop up the filth, drop it down the hatch, and batten down the lid. Plenty of ancient evils lurked in the Deep Down, their senses attuned to the smallest openings to our world. Human history was dotted with near misses, thanks in part to the vigilance of my lineage.

The thought of being the one to screw up that streak was hell on a good night's sleep, let me tell you.

At Avenue C, I rounded a small mountain of plowed trash and shuffled to a stop. A new scent was skewering the vaporous reek, hooking like a talon in my throat. A sickly-sweet scent, like crushed cockroach or…

Fear spread through me as I raised my eyes toward the source: a steep apartment building with a pair of lights burning near the top floor. Dark magic dissipated above the building in a blood-red haze.

I *was* too late. And whatever the conjurer had summoned was no cockroach.

"Crap," I spat, and launched into a run.

The smell was distinctly demonic.

2

I stumbled into a blacked-out lobby, raised my ironwood cane, and uttered, *"Illuminare."*

White light swelled from an opal inset in the cane's end to reveal an upended concierge's desk and graffiti-smeared walls. The single elevator door opposite me was open. I moved toward it, noting the message sprayed over the burned-out elevator lights: "STEP RIGHT IN," with an arrow inviting riders into a carless shaft. I peeked down the two-story plunge to a subbasement, where I could hear something large thump-dragging around.

No thanks.

I hit the stairwell and took the steps two at a time. The cloying smell from the street sharpened in my sinuses, making my eyes water. I had smelled demon before, but in Eastern Europe, years ago—the near-death experience had marked my passage into wizardhood, in a way.

But no, never here. Not in New York.

Which meant a seriously evil conjurer had slipped under the Order's watchful gaze. I considered sending up a message, but that would take energy I couldn't afford at the moment—

not to mention time. The Oracular Order of Magi and Magical Beings was an esteemed and ancient body. Accordingly, they made decisions at a pace on par with the Mendenhall glacier.

That, and I was still on their iffy list for what had happened ten years earlier, during the aforementioned demonic encounter. Never mind that my actions (which, okay, *had* involved summoning an incubus spirit) saved my life, or that I was only twenty-two at the time.

So yeah, the less contact with the Order, the better, I'd since learned.

Between the third and fourth floors, the stairwell began to vibrate. At the fifth floor—the one on which I'd observed the lights from outside—the vibrating became a hammering. I pulled the stairwell door open onto a stink of hard diesel and understood the commotion's source: a gas-powered generator. At the hallway's end, light outlined a door.

I was halfway to the door when a woman's scream pierced the tumult. Jerking my cane into two parts, I gripped a staff in my left hand and a steel sword in my right. A shadow grew around the door a second before it banged open.

The man was six foot ten, easy. Blades of black tattooing scaled his pin-pierced face, giving over to an all-out ink fight on his shaved scalp. Leather and spiked studs stretched over powerful arms holding what looked like a pump-action shotgun.

The sorcerer's bodyguard?

He inclined forward, squinting into the dim hallway. The screaming behind him continued, accompanied now by angry beats and the wail of a guitar. I exhaled and sheathed my sword.

Punks. The literal kind.

"Hey!" Tattoo Face boomed as I retreated back toward the

stairwell. "You're missing a kickass set. Blade's only on till two." Then as a further inducement: "Half cover, since you got here late."

I sniffed the air, but the generator's fumes were still clouding over the demon smell. I couldn't fix on a direction. I returned to Tattoo Face, shouting to be heard. "Do you live here?"

He shrugged as he lowered the shotgun. "Live. Squat."

"Seen anyone strange in the building?" I peered past him into the hazy room of head-bangers, the pink-haired singer/screamer—Blade, I presumed—standing on the hearth of a bricked-over fireplace. I decided to rephrase the question. "Anyone who looks like they don't belong?"

Behind all of his ink, the punk's face was surprisingly soft, almost boyish, but it hardened as I stepped more fully into the generator-powered light. I followed his gaze down to where my tweed jacket and dark knit tie peeked from the parting flaps of my trench coat. Beneath his own jacket, he was wearing a bandolier of shotgun shells.

"You a narc or something?" he asked.

I shook my head. "Just looking for someone."

His eyes fell further to my walking cane, which, not to polish my own brass, was at definite odds with someone six feet tall and in his apparent prime. My hairline had receded slightly, but still... Tattoo Face frowned studiously, as though still undecided if he could trust me.

"I help people," I added.

After another moment, he nodded. "Strange guy showed up a couple of weeks ago. Hauled a big trunk upstairs." He raised his eyes. "Unit right above ours. Talks to himself. Same things, over and over."

I sprinted back to the stairwell, not bothering with the

usual pretense of a trick knee to explain the cane. Tattoo Face seemed not to notice.

"Blade's on till two!" he shouted after me.

I raised a hand in thanks for the reminder, but I was still mulling the *talks to himself* part. The *over and over* sounded like chanting.

Add them up and I'd found my conjurer.

3

O n the sixth floor, the demon stink was back. And gut-rottingly potent. I called more light to my cane and advanced on the door at hallway's end, weathered floor-boards creaking underfoot.

The knob turned in my grasp, but one or more bolts were engaged. Crouching, I sniffed near the dark door space and immediately regretted the decision. "Holy *hell*," I whispered against my coat sleeve. The sickly-sweet scent burned all the way up to my brain, like ammonia.

Drawing the sword from my cane, I pointed it at the door and uttered, *"Vigore."*

A force shot down the length of the blade and snapped the bolts. The door blew inward. With another incantation, the light from my staff slid into a curved shield. I crouched, ready for anything, but except for the vibrating coming from one floor down, the space beyond the door was still and silent.

I tested the threshold with the tip of my sword. It broke the plane cleanly, which meant no warding spells.

Odd...

I entered, sword and glowing staff held forward. The unit was a restored tenement that, like many in the East Village, had been written off in the Crash's rumbling wake and left to die. Shadows climbed and fell over a newspaper-littered living room. I crept past sticks of curb-side furniture and a spill of canned goods before ducking beneath a line of hanging boxer briefs, still damp.

Hardly the evil-sorcerer sanctum I'd imagined.

I stuck my light into one of the doorless bedrooms, the silence tense against my eardrums. A thin roll-up mattress lay slipshod on a metal bed frame, dirty sheets puddled around its legs. A cracked window framed the bombed-out ruin of a neighboring building. When a pipe coughed, I wheeled, my gaze falling to a crowded plank-and-cinderblock bookcase.

In the light of my staff, I scanned book spines that might as well have read "Amateur Conjurer." Abrahamic texts, including a Bible, gave way to dime-store spell books and darker tomes, but without organization. Spaghetti shots in the dark. Someone looking for power or answers.

So where had the demon come from? More crucially, where had it gone?

In the neighboring bedroom, I flinched as my gaze met my own hazel eyes in a mirror on the near wall. *Gonna give myself a fricking heart attack.* Opposite the mirror, an oblong table held a scatter of spell-cooking implements. A Bunsen burner stood on one end, its line snaking to a tipped-over propane tank. Beside the tank, a pair of legs protruded.

I rounded the table and knelt beside the fallen conjurer. Parting a spill of dark, greasy hair, I took in a middle-aged male face with Coke-bottle glasses that had fallen askew, magnifying his whiskered right cheek. I recognized some of the conjurers in the city—or thought I did—and I'd never seen this guy. I straightened his glasses and patted his cheek firmly.

"*Hey*," I whispered.

The man choked on a snort, then fell back into his mind-shattered slumber. He was alive, anyway.

I raised my light to the protective circle the man had chalked on the floorboards and no doubt stood inside while casting his summoning spell. A common mistake. Chalk made fragile circles. And a circle only protected spell casters capable of instilling them with power. That excluded most mortals, who weren't designed to channel, much less direct, the ley energies of this world.

They can damn sure act as gateways to other worlds, though.

My gaze shifted to a second circle near the table's far end, this one with a crude pentagram drawn inside. From a toppled pile of ash and animal entrails, a glistening residue slid into an adjacent bathroom.

Crap.

I felt quickly beneath the man's army surplus jacket and exhaled as my hand came back dry. The only reason he wasn't dead or mortally wounded was the recentness of the spell. Demonic creatures summoned from deeper down underwent a period of gestation, usually in a dark, damp space, to fortify their strength. They emerged half blind, drawn by the scent of the conjurer's vital organs, from which they derived even more potency.

That I'd arrived before that had happened was to my advantage. I hoped.

Rising, I crept toward the bathroom.

4

The trail turned dark red over the bathroom's dingy tiles, gobbets of black matter glistening in its wake. By now I was more or less desensitized to the smell, thank God. Through the half-open door, my light shone over a dripping faucet. The end of a free-standing tub glowed beyond.

With a foot, I edged the door wider.

The trail climbed the side of the tub, spread into a foul puddle, then climbed again. This time into a torn-out section of tiling between the shower head and the hot and cold spigots down below.

I adjusted my slick grip on the sword handle. The creature was inside the wall.

My sword hummed as I channeled currents of ley energy. With a *"Vigore!"* I thrust the sword toward the hole.

Tile and plaster exploded over my light shield in a dusty wave. A keening cry went up. In the exposed wall, wedged behind oozing pipes, I saw it. The creature had enfolded its body with a pair of membranous black wings. From a skull-sharp head of bristling hair, a pair of albino-white eyes stared blindly. Before I could push the attack, the creature screamed again.

The jagged sound became a weapon. Waves as sharp as the creature's barbed teeth pierced my thoughts and fractured my casting prism. I was dealing with a shrieker. A lower demonic being but ridiculously deadly—even to wizards.

My light shield wavered in front of me, then burst in a shower of sparks. The energetic release thrust me backwards as the room fell dark, my right heel catching the threshold. A squelch sounded, followed by the shallow splash of the thing dropping into the tub.

I flailed for balance but went down. My right elbow slammed into the floor, sending a numbing bolt up and down my arm. When metal clanged off behind me, I realized I'd lost my sword.

Beyond my outstretched legs, claws scrabbled over porcelain.

I kick-scooted away, sweeping an arm back for my weapon.

Wings slapped the air, the wet sound swallowed by the shrieker's next cry. Abandoning my search, I thrust my staff into the darkness above my face. The end struck something soft. A claw hooked behind my right orbital bone before tearing away, missing my eyeball by a breath.

I felt the shrieker flap past me, still clumsy in its just-summoned state. No doubt going for the conjurer. But if I was going to stop it, I had to do something about the damned screaming.

Blood dribbled down the side of my face as I sat up. Praying the shrieker wasn't rounding back on me, I jammed a finger into each ear. With the screaming muted, I repeated a centering mantra. Within seconds, the mental prism through which I converted ley energy into force and light reconstituted. A white orb swelled from the end of my staff, illuminating the apartment once more. I quickly touched the staff to each ear, uttering Words of Power. Shields of light energy covered them like muffs, blocking out the shrieker's cries.

I scooped up my sword and raised both sword and staff, expecting to find the shrieker hunched over the splayed-out conjurer. But the conjurer was alone, the shrieker nowhere in sight. The animal entrails were missing from the summoning circle, though, meaning it had fed.

Not good.

I raised my light toward the windows to ensure they were still intact. Remembering the blown-open front door, I hurried to the main room, terrified the creature had gotten out and into the city's six-million-person buffet. I ducked beneath the clothesline and felt the newspapers at my feet gusting up. I spun to find the abomination flapping at my face.

"Vigore!" I cried.

The wave-like force from my sword blasted the shrieker into a corner of the ceiling. It dropped onto a radiator, then tumbled wetly to the floor. I repeated the Word, but the shrieker scrabbled behind a wooden chair and darted into the bedroom. The chair blew apart in its stead.

I pursued and, guessing the creature's next move, aimed my staff at the near window. *"Protezione!"*

The light shield that spread over the glass held long enough for the shrieker to bounce from it. The shrieker launched itself at the window beside it, but I cast first. More sparks fell away as it beat its wings up and down the protected window like a flailing moth.

"You're not going anywhere, you little imp."

Only it wasn't so little anymore. The bed jumped when the shrieker dropped onto the headboard, taloned feet gripping the metal bar. The white caul over its eyes was thinning, too, goat-like pupils peering out. As I crept nearer, the creature's appearance stirred in me equal parts fascination and revulsion. Its wings spread to reveal a wrinkled body mapped in throbbing black vessels.

Okay, now it was just revulsion.

The shrieker put everything into its next scream. The light energy over my right ear broke apart. A sensation like shattered glass filled my head. Hunching my shoulder to my naked ear, I threw my weight into a sword thrust and grunted as hot fluid sprayed over me.

The shrieker fell silent, staring at me as though trying to comprehend what I had done. Its eyes fell to the sword, which had skewered its chest and driven a solid inch into the wall behind it. But it wasn't enough to physically wound such creatures. They had to be dispersed.

"*Disfare*," I shouted, concentrating force along the blade.

The shrieker's wings trembled, then began to flail. Unfortunately, the more power it took to summon a creature into our world, the more power it required to send it back. And the homeless appearance of the conjurer aside, some damned powerful magic had called this thing up.

"*Disfare!*" I repeated, louder.

The shrieker thrashed more fiercely, the tarry fluid that bubbled from its mouth drowning its hideous cry. But its form remained intact. And I was pushing my limits, a lead-like fatigue beginning to weigh on my limbs. The shrieker's wings folded down, and a pair of bat-like hands seized the blade.

"What the...?"

The creature gave a pull and skewered itself toward me.

"Hey, stop that!" I yelled pointlessly.

I pressed my glowing staff against its chin, but with another tug, the shrieker was an inch closer. It snapped at my staff with gunky teeth, then swiped with a clawed hand, narrowly missing my reared-back face.

I considered ditching my sword, but then what? I wasn't dealing with flesh and blood here. The second the shrieker came off the hilt, it would reconfigure itself, becoming larger and more powerful. And if it overwhelmed me, the conjurer would be next, followed by the head-bangers one floor down. An image of the party as a bloody scene of carnage jagged through my mind's eye.

"DISFARE!" I boomed.

A tidal wave of energy burst from my mental prism, shook down the length of my arm, through my sword, and then out the creature. I squeezed my eyes closed as the creature's gargling shriek cut off and an explosion of foul-smelling phlegm nearly knocked me down.

There was a reason I'd waterproofed my coat, and it wasn't for the shiny look.

I opened my eyes to a steamy, tar-spattered room and exhaled. The shrieker was gone, cast back to its hellish pit.

But at a price.

The edges of my thoughts swam in creamy waves, a sensation that heralded the impending arrival of Thelonious. That incubus spirit I called up a decade ago? He was still around, clinging to my spirit like a parasite. Despite that he was thousands of years old, I pictured him as a cool cat in black shades and a glittering 'fro—probably because he shared a name with a famous musician. And my Thelonious had a jazzy way about him. As long as I didn't push my limits, I could keep him at bay. Cross that line, and I became a vessel for Thelonious's, ahem, festivities.

And yeah, I'd just crossed that line.

More creamy waves washed in. I would have to work quickly.

The demonic gunk was evaporating as I drew my sword from the wall. I cleaned the blade against the thigh of my coat, resheathed it, and then returned to the fallen conjurer. Still out. I shone my light over his table, pocketing samples of spell ingredients for later study.

"But where oh where is the recipe?" I muttered.

I stopped at the flaky ashes of what appeared to have been a piece of college-ruled paper. The spell must have contained an incineration component, meant to destroy evidence of its origin.

"Naturally."

Sliding my cane into the belt of my coat, I stooped for the conjurer. "Up you go," I grunted. His head lolled as I carried him into the bedroom. I set him on the mattress, arranged his arms and legs into a semblance of order, then shook out the sheet and spread it over him.

His mortal mind was blown, but not beyond repair.

I touched my cane to the center of his brow and uttered ancient Words of healing. He murmured as a cottony light grew from the remaining power in the staff. The healing would take time, which was just as well. In a few more minutes, I wouldn't be in much shape to question him.

"I'll be back in a couple of days," I told the snoring man.

The creamy waves crested, spilling into my final wells of free will. There was no good place to go now except away from people. I was turning to leave when my—or I should say, Thelonious's—gaze fell to the space beneath the bed. A half-full bottle of tannic liquid leaned against one of the legs.

I felt my lips stretch into a grin. *Bourbon*, Thelonious purred in his bass voice.

My final memory of that night, the fire of alcohol in my throat, was tottering down a hallway toward a shaking generator and the siren screams of a pink-haired punker named Blade.

Ooh, yeah...

As a scholar and spell-caster, Everson Croft knows his magic. But when a mysterious evil threatens New York City, will it be enough?

AUTHOR'S NOTES

First, thanks for reading *Book of Souls*!

As a short prequel to *Demon Moon*, I thought it would be fun to pay homage to the gothic horror genre. Not only had novels like Stoker's *Dracula* and Shelley's *Frankenstein* fascinated me as a teen, they would ultimately inform the urban fantasy genre that I love so much today.

So pay homage I did. Hence the ominous weather, superstitious village, haunted "castle"—in this case, monastery—replete with secret rooms, and of course the naïve young man from the city (sorry, Everson). No damsel in distress, though. Or at least *true* distress. Wink, wink.

I also needed to crack the whip and make the prequel do some work. Sure enough, *Book of Souls* sets up important story elements for the series. Everson's incubus problem being one. But the scenes between Everson and his grandfather are especially key—and will make a lot more sense as the books progress, I promise!

The adventures of Everson (and Tabitha) pick up in *Demon Moon, Prof Croft Book 1*, now part of five-book box set.

I sincerely hope you'll continue the journey.

Best wishes,
Brad

P.S. Be sure to check out my website to learn more about the Croftverse, download another prequel, and find out what's coming! That's all at bradmagnarella.com

CROFTVERSE CATALOGUE

PROF CROFT PREQUELS

Book of Souls

Siren Call

MAIN SERIES

Demon Moon

Blood Deal

Purge City

Death Mage

Black Luck

Power Game

Druid Bond

Night Rune

Shadow Duel

Shadow Deep

Godly Wars

Angel Doom

SPIN-OFFS

Croft & Tabby

Croft & Wesson

BLUE WOLF

Blue Curse

Blue Shadow

Blue Howl

Blue Venom

Blue Blood

Blue Storm

SPIN-OFF

Legion Files

———————

For the entire chronology go to bradmagnarella.com

ABOUT THE AUTHOR

Brad Magnarella writes good-guy urban fantasy for the same reason most read it...

To explore worlds where magic crackles from fingertips, vampires and shifters walk city streets, cats talk (some excessively), and good prevails against all odds. It's shamelessly fun.

His two main series, Prof Croft and Blue Wolf, make up the growing Croftverse, with over a quarter-million books sold to date and an Independent Audiobook Award nomination.

Hopelessly nomadic, Brad can be found in a rented room overseas or hiking America's backcountry.

Or just go to www.bradmagnarella.com

Made in the USA
Coppell, TX
14 January 2024

27645979R00073